DARK DREAM

DARK DREAM

BY

DAPHNE CLAIR

MILLS & BOON LIMITED
ETON HOUSE, 18-24 PARADISE ROAD,
RICHMOND, SURREY TW9 1SR

MILLS & BOON and Rose Device is registered in US Patent and Trademark Office

First published in Great Britain 1985 by Mills & Boon Limited

© Daphne Clair 1985

*Australian copyright 1985
Philippine copyright 1985
Reprinted 1985
Large Print edition 1987*

ISBN 0 263 11564 X

*Set in Monotype Times 16 on 16.5 pt.
16-0886-52887*

*Typeset in Great Britain by
Associated Publishing Services Ltd
Printed and bound in Great Britain by
William Clowes, Beccles, Suffolk*

CHAPTER ONE

SHE had been asleep on the daisy-dusted grass under the old puriri. She lay with her eyes still closed, listening to the sounds of summer—the distant bleat of a sheep, a lark threading its song into the sky, cicadas thrumming in chorus, and the faint whisper of a passing breeze stirring the leaves overhead.

A slight rustling of the grass beside her made her aware that she was not alone, but before she could open her eyes she felt the shadow of someone leaning over her, and warm lips brushed hers.

Happiness flooded her, and she returned the kiss instantly, eagerly, her lips clinging when it seemed he would have moved away, curving her arms around his shoulders, spreading her hands on a sun-warmed cotton shirt, keeping her eyes tightly closed as his mouth suddenly hardened on hers and the kiss deepened.

It had never been quite like this before, but they had been apart for so long, and this time he was home for good, wasn't he? The long years of waiting were over. He coaxed her mouth open, and her breathing quickened as desire unfolded inside her. Her body went taut and she thought that for a moment he held his breath, before the kiss became gentler, soft and drugging.

When at last he drew away she opened her eyes lazily, smiling, saying drowsily, 'Michael.'

Then she jack-knifed into a sitting position, staring in disbelief at the blond man who sat with his forearm resting on one raised knee, his blue eyes regarding her with a peculiarly intense light in them, and a hint of colour behind the faint tan on his high cheekbones.

She gasped, *'Simon!'*

'Yes,' he said calmly. 'Simon.'

'I thought it was Michael!'

'Yes, I know.'

'Well——'

He smiled at her as she floundered to a stop. 'Well?' he repeated.

'Well—what on earth did you kiss me for?' she demanded.

He laughed, throwing back his head. 'My dear Meredith,' he said, 'why does any man

kiss a pretty girl? Anyway, it's the accepted
way of awakening a sleeping beauty, isn't it?
I couldn't resist, that's all. Though I must
admit I hadn't intended to be quite so—
thorough-going about it. I do think you must
take some of the blame for that.'

'I told you, I thought it was Michael!'

'Ah.'

She wasn't sure what he meant by that,
but it seemed to denote some sort of under-
standing. 'You could have stopped me!' she
said with indignant reproach.

'Now why should I want to do that?' he
asked reasonably. 'I was enjoying it far too
much—I thought you were, too.'

Her face flamed. 'But I wasn't kissing *you*!'

The laughter in his face died. 'No,' he said
slowly. 'I see. I'm sorry if I offended you,
Meredith. I didn't think you'd mind. After
all, we're good friends, aren't we?'

'Yes,' she answered somewhat grudgingly.
'Of course we are,' she added with something
like relief. He had only meant it as a light
peck, but she had responded so quickly to
the kiss she had thought was Michael's, she
couldn't really blame him for taking advantage of it. Only it was unsettling to have

Simon, of all people, looking at her the way he had afterwards; and when she thought of how his mouth had so intimately explored hers . . .

For the first time she wondered if Simon had girlfriends. He must miss his wife, and he was a good-looking man and still young, after all. In his early thirties, she supposed. He had been twenty-two when he and Jill got married. Meredith remembered the wedding—Jill looking stunningly beautiful in bridal white that accentuated her silver blonde hair and creamy skin, and Simon almost as fair as his wife, terribly handsome in a dark suit and white shirt, so that thirteen-year-old Meredith had felt the delicious pangs of her first fleeting teenage 'crush'. It hadn't occurred to her before that Simon was handsome. He had just been the much older brother of her best friend, Anneke Van Dyk, whose Dutch-born parents, with their large family, lived on the farm across the road from her home. She had not seen quite so much of him after his marriage, until Jill died and he had brought his baby son home to his parents for them to look after, since when he had spent virtually every weekend there.

In four years Benjy had grown into a sturdy little boy, a favourite not only with his grandparents and his six aunts and uncles, but with Meredith and her parents as well. Simon had become a friend of the family. And it was silly to mind him kissing her. He hadn't meant it as anything more than a teasing gesture, an impulse of the moment, as he had explained, and if she had only opened her eyes in time that's what it would have remained.

He reached over and took her hand. 'Forgive me?' he asked, smiling at her, his head on one side, his eyes amused.

'Yes, of course,' she said.

He didn't let go of her hand, but sat looking apparently absentmindedly at the slim fingers held in his. 'Michael rates a kiss like that, does he, Meredith?' he asked her.

'He's been away a long time. I've missed him.'

Simon looked straight into her eyes then, his own eyes questioning. 'And . . . ?' he probed gently.

'And we love each other,' Meredith confessed, prompted partly by the insistence in his voice, partly by a desire to share her happiness.

'I see.' Simon released her hand and smiled at her again. 'And he's just been waiting to get his degree before you announce it to the world, has he?'

'Something like that.'

'I hadn't realised. I know you've spent some time with him in the university holidays, of course. But you're friendly with his sister, aren't you? And he isn't the only young man I've seen you with.'

'I've gone out with other boys, sometimes, but they're just friends. And I only did it because he didn't want me to feel tied to him while he was away. And also partly because my parents seemed to think I ought to know some other men before I settle down. But it's only Michael who counts.'

'Lucky Michael,' Simon said quietly. 'He's about the same age as you, isn't he?'

'A year older. He's already twenty-three.'

'I'm eight years older than that.'

'Really?' she said vaguely, because the remark seemed irrelevant.

'Yes, really,' He seemed to be laughing at her again with his eyes. 'Does it seem ancient to you?'

'Of course not. Simon . . . have you ever thought of marrying again?'

For some reason his smile had a wry twist, and she was sorry she had asked because a sadness came into his eyes. 'The thought did cross my mind,' he said. 'But it isn't so easy . . . '

'You mean, you couldn't love anyone as you did Jill?'

'Perhaps,' he said. 'Something like that.'

'You did love her very much, didn't you?' she asked softly. 'I remember how you were, together.' They had always seemed to be bathed in sunlight, the two of them wrapped in a glowing golden cocoon, both so fair, good looking and vital and so much in love, even after they had been married for several years. She had liked visiting Anneke and her family when they were there. Everyone about them seemed to become more alive, and the house always rang with laughter.

'Yes,' he said quietly. 'I did love her very much. I hope that life will be as good to you, Meredith, and for much, much longer.'

'Thank you, Simon.' She was touched. It was a lovely wish, and she knew it was sincere.

'Your mother sent me to fetch you,' he told her. 'Mrs Kingsley phoned a while ago to say that Michael's arrived from Auckland. They're coming over for afternoon tea.'

'He's *here*? Why didn't you *say* so!' She began scrambling to her feet, and he offered a hand, saying, 'Don't panic. They're on their way, that's all.'

'Oh, heck, my hair! And my jeans!' She frantically pushed back her long, straight brown hair with two hands, and then dusted the seat of her denims. 'And I'll have grass and stuff all over my back!' She tried to twist her head to look over her shoulder.

'Turn around,' Simon ordered. 'I'll brush you down.'

'Oh, thank you.' Gratefully she obeyed, and felt his fingers picking bits off her pink T-shirt, then brushing at the fabric. 'You've got a twig in your hair,' he said. 'Hold still a minute.'

She felt several small tugs and then he tossed the twisted little scrap to the grass and brought her round to face him, his hands firm on her shoulders. 'You look beautiful,' he said, looking into her anxious brown eyes. 'Don't worry.' He paused. 'The kiss I stole was Michael's, it seems. Do you think you could spare another one, for my very own?'

He was smiling so nicely at her, what else could she do? But she felt a strange reluctance as she steadied herself with her hands on his shoulders and put her lips to his, and she made it very brief. If he was disappointed he didn't show it, merely taking her hand to lead her into the sunlight, up the gentle slope of the paddock where she scorned his help to climb the fence at the corner, through the old orchard and across the lawn to the square, red-roofed farm house.

They were half-way there when she saw the dark blue car parked in front of the house, and cried out, 'They're here!'

She tugged her hand from his light clasp and began to run, her hair streaming behind her. It wasn't until she reached the wide verandah that went round the front and two sides of the house that she stopped, waiting for Simon, who had quickened his pace but still lagged behind. He was, after all, a visitor, and she knew she ought not to have left him.

'I'm sorry,' she said, panting slightly. 'It's just——'

'I know, it's been a long time and you can't

wait.'

'You are *nice*, Simon!'

Again that odd wryness appeared in his smile. 'I suspect you think everyone is nice at the moment, and all the world is wonderful. Isn't that right?'

'Maybe.' A smile of pure joy tugged at her lips. Suddenly for some odd reason she was nervous about going in. 'Do you think I should change?' she asked him. 'Put on a dress or something?'

'I told you,' he said patiently, 'you look just fine. Come on, I suppose Michael's just as eager as you are for this meeting. Don't keep him on tenterhooks any longer.'

They went in together, pausing inside the door of the front room, which seemed overfull of people: her mother and father, Michael's parents and his sister Debra, Simon's son Benjy sitting with his ten-year-old youngest uncle, and a young woman she didn't know. And Michael.

Her eyes found him, his slight, wiry figure, his black curly hair, his warm hazel eyes looking at her with an expression she couldn't fathom.

'Michael!' she said. She wanted to cross

the room and fling herself into his arms, but something held her back, shyness or a strange kind of premonition.

And her mother said loudly, 'Well, Michael's home again, and he's brought a surprise this time, Meredith. This,' she indicated the young woman Meredith had hardly noticed, 'is Francine Gregory, Michael's fiancée.'

Meredith's eyes swivelled to her mother's face, saw some desperate message behind the determined pleased smile, and at first the words didn't make sense. *She* was Michael's fiancée—or as good as—she was Michael's girl, since they had both been at high school. He might not formally have asked her to marry him, but it had always been understood, hadn't it? She looked at Michael, and although he was trying to hide it, she saw the same look of desperate anxiety in his eyes as in her mother's. The room took on a surreal quality, the people in it appeared to be moving in slow motion, like a film, and she herself seemed as detached as a watcher in the stalls. None of it had anything to do with her. The world receded.

Then she heard her own voice speaking in

a disembodied fashion, saying, 'But Michael, you can't——'

She stopped, because Simon, standing beside her, had suddenly put his arm about her and was gripping her upper arm so hard that the pain brought reality back with it. Overriding her voice, he said, 'Well, congratulations, Michael. That's wonderful, isn't it, darling?' He looked down at her, and she raised dark eyes to his face, with the strange impression that he had willed her to look at him. Then, holding her eyes with his, he said, 'And *we* have some news, too. Not ten minutes ago, Meredith consented to be my wife.'

Her mouth fell open, and he swooped and kissed her hard, silencing her amazed protest. When he had finished, brief though the kiss had been, she was beyond speech. The whole chain of events was so crazy it couldn't really be happening, anyway. She must be still lying under the puriri having an idiotic dream. Fatalistically she decided to see what happened next. Anyway, she felt rather sick. The babel of astonished voices that had broken out seemed far away. Then her mother's face came into focus as she hugged

Meredith, her eyes still worried but her smile less artificial. Her father was shaking Simon's free hand—his other arm still held her, and she was grateful because her knees felt as if they weren't there any more, and she didn't want to fall down, and it was important not to make a fool of herself, although she couldn't quite recall why . . .

Michael came up to her and said something, and she saw his pleased smile and the relief in his eyes and he kissed her cheek and then all she could see was a whirling kaleidoscope of spots before her eyes getting darker and darker, and someone said, 'Are you all right?'

She heard herself say quite clearly, 'I think I'm going to faint,' and then she was lifted in strong arms, and Simon's voice was saying, 'I kept her out in the sun too long, and then she would insist on running back here, she wanted to tell you our news.'

For some reason she had a weird desire to giggle, and she tried to say to him, 'Simon, what a liar you are!' But her tongue felt thick and she couldn't get any sound out. Then for a few minutes the blackness took over, and she let herself slide gratefully away into it.

She came to on her own bed, with Simon and her mother bending over her, her mother's hand holding a wet cloth to her forehead.

'Oh, no,' she murmured. 'I made an idiot of myself, didn't I?'

'Of course not,' Simon contradicted. 'There's nothing idiotic about being unwell. You only fainted.'

'Excitement, and a bit too much sun,' Mrs Townsend diagnosed. 'I must say, you've given us all a surprise, you two.'

'I'm sorry,' Meredith murmured, and felt tears slipping down her cheeks on to the pillow. She suddenly realised that she had never been so miserable in her life, and remembered why. Apparently it wasn't a dream, after all. It was all too horribly real.

'Now, then,' her mother wiped at the tears with the cloth. 'Nothing to cry about, Merrie. We're very fond of Simon, and little Benjy. We couldn't be more pleased.'

Meredith choked and turned her face away, encountering Simon's hand somehow with hers and clinging to it like a lifeline.

Her mother said, 'Darling, what is it?' And she buried her face in the pillow as Simon answered smoothly, 'As you said, Mrs Townsend, excitement and too much sun. Why don't you go back to your guests—I can look after Meredith. And when she's feeling a bit better, we have a lot to talk about.'

'Oh. Well, yes, I suppose so,' Mrs Townsend said in somewhat bewildered tones. 'I'll just get her a cup of tea, first.'

When she had brought it she took the cloth and wrung it out again in cold water while Meredith drank the tea. 'Will you be all right now, darling?' she asked, taking the cup and replacing the cool cloth as Meredith sank back on the pillow again.

Meredith nodded, realising that she couldn't talk to Simon with her mother there. And talk to him she must. Physically she was feeling a lot better, but her mind was whirling, in a state of total confusion.

She lay still for a few more minutes after her mother had left, trying to collect her thoughts. She realised that her hand was still in Simon's and made a move to pull away, but his fingers tightened fractionally and she gave up. It was rather nice to have him to hold on to. Her world had suddenly become unstable, an unpredictable place where the impossible happened, and very cold. At least he felt solid and warm and real. After a while she took away the cloth and put it on the bedside table, and said slowly and carefully, 'Simon, I didn't agree to be your wife, did I?'

He smiled down at her with what looked remarkably like tenderness. 'No, Meredith, you didn't.'

'Then why,' she asked, even more slowly and carefully, 'did you say that I had?'

He maintained a thoughtful silence for several seconds, and then said, 'I suppose it was another impulsive act.'

'Like kissing me?'

'Yes. Exactly like that.'

'I don't understand,' she said flatly. 'You don't want to marry me, do you?'

Again he didn't answer straight away. Then finally he asked, 'Would that be so surprising?'

'Yes! Especially since I'd just told you ten minutes ago that I was in love with—with Michael,' she finished in a wobbly whisper.

'Don't cry,' he said softly.

'No, I won't,' she promised, swallowing hard. She wanted to, heaven knew she did, but somewhere inside her there was also a growing anger that scorned the weaker urge. Her brain beginning to function, she stared at him and said, wondering, 'Is that why you did it? To save my pride?'

'More or less,' he admitted. 'You seemed about to say something that you might have regretted a great deal, later. It was all I could think of to prevent you, on the spur of the moment.'

She chewed that over. 'Well, it was pretty brilliant for the spur of the moment,' she told him. 'But what'll we do now? You can't marry me just to stop me from looking silly.'

'We're not married yet,' he reminded her. 'Just engaged.'

'Yes.' She bit her lip, thinking. 'And engagements can be broken.'

'That's right,' he agreed coolly. 'They can.'

'I'm awfully grateful,' she said. 'But doesn't it put you in an awkward position?'

'Why? I'm free and unattached. And you will make a charming fiancée.'

'Even if it's only temporary?'

Again he let a small silence elapse. 'Even then,' he agreed. 'And please don't think you have to be grateful. I may have an ulterior motive.'

'I can't imagine what it might be,' she said. 'You're just making that up.'

'Am I?' For a moment his eyes cooled, looking almost angry, and she thought with a shock that she wouldn't want to be on the wrong side of Simon, although he had never been less than extremely pleasant to her. 'Don't be too sure,' he added.

It sounded, oddly, almost like a warning.

CHAPTER TWO

AFTER a while Simon suggested quietly, 'Do you feel ready to go back to the sitting room again? Your colour looks pretty normal, now.'

She felt herself trying to shrink back against the pillows, her face tightening. He said gently, 'You'll have to face him sometime, Meredith. It may be easier with your family about you—and I'll be there, too.'

Somehow that made it better, and she took a couple of quick breaths and said, 'Yes. All right.'

He smiled. 'Good girl.'

She let him help her up off the bed although the sick dizziness had quite gone. Pushing a strand of hair from her forehead she said, 'I'd better comb my hair—tidy myself a bit.'

'Shall I go?' he asked.

'No, please,' she said jerkily. She didn't want to be alone just yet. She went to the dressing table and picked up the hairbrush. Smoothing back the long tresses, she glanced in the mirror and saw that Simon was

watching her intently. Her eyes skittered away
from him. There was something intimate
about brushing her hair in front of a man in
her own bedroom. She stopped abruptly and
fumbled in the little blue china box for two
clips to hold her hair back from her temples.
There was a lipstick in the box too. She
hardly ever wore make-up—her clear skin
tanned easily to golden brown in the summer
and she didn't like the sticky feeling of
lipstick. But now her mouth looked pale and
pinched, and she quickly applied some colour,
biting on a tissue to blot it. Luckily her eyes
showed almost no traces of tears, only
perhaps a hint of extra lustre. She'd do.

She turned to face Simon. 'All set?' he
asked. And when she nodded and came over
to him, he added, 'Now, smile.'

She obliged with an effort, and he put out
his hand, taking hers into its warm clasp.
'That's right,' he said. 'Chin up, darling.'

She held his hand tightly when they re-
entered the sitting room, and managed to
keep the smile on her face while she assured
everyone she was quite recovered thank you,
and yes she supposed she shouldn't have run
in this heat immediately after a nap, and

she'd be careful not to do it again.

'You haven't met Francine properly,' Michael's father said, and she went rigid, but Simon's fingers squeezed hers and he compelled her to go with him as he crossed the room to where Michael's fiancée was sitting on the window seat with him. They were holding hands too, and for a moment Meredith couldn't tear her eyes away from their entwined fingers. Then she forced herself to look at the girl's face, getting an impression of sandy curls, an attractively freckled nose, and a friendly smile. 'Are you sure you're okay?' Francine asked. 'You don't need to drag yourself out for me, you know.'

'I'm fine,' Meredith heard herself say. In other circumstances she would probably have liked Francine. 'I—don't think I congratulated you two properly. How—how long have you been engaged?'

'Oh, it's very recent,' the girl laughed. 'Only a couple of days. A real whirlwind romance, wasn't it, Michael?'

'I guess so,' Michael agreed. 'We'd both been at the university for years, and yet we only met in the last few weeks. Hard to believe isn't it? And then, when the end of the year came, I realised I couldn't leave without making sure this girl came with me. So I popped the question, and she said yes.'

'What about you two?' Francine enquired. 'I gather you've known each other for a bit longer?'

'A long time,' Simon confirmed. 'I've watched Meredith growing up, but it wasn't until today that I realised I was in love with her. And——' he added, smiling down at her, '—apparently she feels the same.'

He really sounded awfully convincing, she thought, as she made an effort to smile back at him in a suitably besotted fashion. Feeling Michael's eyes on her, and sensing puzzlement, she said recklessly to Simon, 'Well, I'd been waiting, you know. If you hadn't asked me soon I think I'd have done the proposing myself.'

She saw the surprise in his eyes before he laughed and kissed her briefly. Then Benjy was tugging at his free hand, asking, 'Daddy, is Merrie better now?'

'Much better,' he answered reassuringly, swinging the little boy up into his arms.

'Then why are you kissing her?'

The other adults laughed, but Simon said

quite seriously, 'Because I love her, son.'

'I love her, too.' Benjy stretched out his arms to Meredith and pressed a warm, moist kiss on her cheek.

'I love you, too, Benjy,' Meredith said, taking him from his father.

'He's too heavy for you,' Simon protested.

But he was wriggling down now, anyway, pulling at Meredith's hand. 'Read the bulldozer story for me, please, Merrie?'

Glad to escape, she complied, taking out the dog-eared book that had once belonged to her older brother from the box of toys her mother kept for visiting children, and settling Benjy with her in one of the armchairs.

The conversation floated about and over them while she read, spinning the story out as much as possible, giving herself a breathing space.

The Kingsleys and Francine were leaving, saying goodbye all around. Francine stopped by Meredith's chair, urging her, 'Don't move, for heaven's sake. It was nice meeting you. I'll see you again, won't I?'

'Of course.' They could hardly avoid it, Meredith realised with a sense of continuing nightmare. Michael, now that he had his law degree, was all set to enter his uncle's firm in Whangarei, their nearest city, as a junior partner. It had been planned for years. His parents and hers had been friends since Meredith's father moved on to his Northland farm twenty years ago. Mr Kingsley had then been manager of the local dairy factory. The Dairy Company had amalgamated with a bigger one, forcing Mr Kingsley into early retirement, and he had bought a house and settled in Whangarei. But the families still saw a lot of each other.

Michael hovered somewhat awkwardly nearby, then leaned over to squeeze her shoulder with his hand. 'All the best, Merrie,' he said. As she looked fleetingly into his eyes she saw again that look of puzzlement she had noticed before. 'I'm very happy for you.'

'And I for you,' she returned, terribly polite. Let you out nicely, didn't it, she thought savagely. The embarrassment might not have been all on her side if she had blurted out that she had thought him promised to *her*. Obviously he hadn't mentioned their long special friendship to Francine. The girl hadn't had an inkling, she was sure.

She heard the car go away, and was hit by a dreadful awareness of finality. Michael was in a sense going out of her life. That was going to leave an awfully big gap, because all her plans and hopes and dreams had centred around him for so long. At school she had done well, choosing to take a basic commercial course because she enjoyed figures and liked typing and was good at it. In her last year she had gained the highest marks in her class in several subjects, and passed external business exams to emerge with very good qualifications. Her parents would have been happy to help her if she had wanted to take a university course in commerce, but it had cost them a lot financing her brother Ian through his degree, and she knew that she was going to marry Michael and have his children to take up her time for a good many years, so although higher education was never wasted, any practical benefit would be very indirect and a long time coming. She had taken some night classes in computer science and accountancy because she enjoyed using her brain and practising new skills, but although the prospect of being at university with Michael was tempting, she didn't think it worthwhile to spend three years learning things she would probably never use.

Almost without trying she had found herself, after starting as a record typist and clerk with the local Hospital Board, promoted through the system until she was now in a senior position, and she knew that if she wanted to move into administration, it wouldn't be difficult. Although young, she was intelligent, interested in her work and extremely accurate. But it was only a stopgap, and she had no real ambition.

The room had become much quieter. Simon came over and said to Benjy, 'Uncle Christopher's going to take you home, son.'

'You come too, Daddy.'

'Later, Ben.' Simon never called his son Benjy. He never used the diminutive of Meredith's name either. 'I want to stay and talk about boring grown-up things with Mr and Mrs Townsend. I'll be home soon.'

Christopher took his nephew's hand and they each got a biscuit from Meredith's mother and a warning to be careful crossing the road. When they had gone, Simon turned to the older couple and said, 'I suppose we ought to apologise for not telling you our news first. I'm afraid that, like Meredith, I was a bit carried away.'

'Don't worry about it, Simon,' Mrs Townsend said warmly. 'We quite understand, and Meredith's over twenty. You don't need our permission.'

'I won't be asking for your prospects,' her husband assured him. 'And we know you well enough to be sure that you'll make a fine husband. You did bef—Well, anyway, we couldn't be happier.'

'Thank you.'

'When do you want to get married?'

Simon smiled easily. 'We haven't got around to discussing that yet. I hope it will be soon.' He transferred the smile to Meredith, whose eyes had widened slightly. He was making it sound so genuine she almost believed in this bogus engagement herself. But surely that had been a mistake? If people expected them to marry soon it didn't give them much time to call it all off convincingly.

Mrs Townsend began collecting up used cups and plates, and Meredith made to help.

'I know it's asking a lot of a girl as young as Meredith to take on a man with a young child,' Simon said to her father. 'You'd probably be happier if she was marrying someone nearer her own age, and without ties of any sort——'

'Not at all,' her father retorted. 'As long as Meredith is happy, that's all we care about. And I don't think she's doing this just because she's sorry for you and fond of Benjy. She's always had a bit of a thing for you—I remember when she was only thirteen she persuaded young Anneke to give her a photograph——'

'*Dad!*' Meredith's cheeks were scarlet.

Her father laughed. 'Swapped your best jersey for it, didn't you?' he recalled. 'I remember your mother being very annoyed about that.'

'Did you, Meredith?' Simon looked intrigued.

'I was only a kid!' she protested. 'It could just as well have been John Travolta or—or Prince Charles!'

'Don't tease her,' Mrs Townsend said to her husband.

'Okay.' Her father relented and came over to kiss her cheek, giving her a hug which made the stack of cups and saucers she was holding wobble dangerously. 'Sorry, lovey. I didn't think you'd mind, now that you're going to marry him. You certainly had your mother and me fooled. We thought you'd got over all that and had your eye on young M— mm—younger men. No offence, Simon, you did say yourself that you're quite a bit older than our girl, here.'

'I did,' Simon agreed equably.

Meredith had a sudden desire to giggle. Her father might not be the most tactful man in the world, but he wasn't usually this bad.

'Well, never mind,' he said now. 'She's got a sensible head on her shoulders, and I'm sure she knows what she's doing. She's pretty mature for her age.'

Simon, she thought, looked as though he might doubt that, and she lifted her chin, a little bit put out. She might be much younger than he, but she was hardly a child.

'Will you stay for tea, Simon?' her mother asked.

'No, thanks, Mrs Townsend. I've promised to help my father with the milking, to give Tony some extra time to swot. He's in the middle of exams.'

'Well, thank your mother for the pears,

won't you? And thanks for bringing them over. Meredith, why don't you give me those cups and walk Simon down to the gate? I expect you two would like some time alone.'

The crockery was taken from her hands, and it seemed she had no option.

The afternoon sun was low in the sky but still hot, and a car passing on the road raised a whirling cloud of dust that settled on the dandelions, wild carrot flowers and tangled blackberries among the tall grass outside the farm fences, and dulled the white plumes of the toi-toi that grew by the gate. Over the road she could see the neat lines of red-leaved photinia bordering the Van Dykes' drive, and a glimpse of the large, comfortable farmhouse behind a shelter of graceful, feathery casuarina. Simon put his arm lightly about her shoulder as they walked. 'I'm sorry to have to go away so soon,' he said, 'but we've weathered the worst of it, I think.'

'I suppose you'll have to tell your parents,' Meredith said unhappily. 'Mum and Dad won't keep quiet.'

'If I know my little brother, Chris will have told them already.'

'Oh, yes. He would have, wouldn't he?'

'Anneke will be thrilled.'

'She'll be surprised!' Anneke knew perfectly well that Michael had filled all of Meredith's emotional life for the past six years. She and Meredith were not best friends for nothing. 'She isn't home this weekend, is she?'

'No, she's on duty at the hospital. You'll see her tomorrow, won't you? Monday?'

'I could. I hate the thought of telling Anneke lies.'

His hand tightened on her shoulder. 'Just tell her we're engaged.'

'But we're not. Not really.'

They had reached the gate, and he turned her into his arms, holding her loosely, his blue eyes meeting her troubled brown ones. 'We could be,' he said.

Meredith shook her head, not under-standing. 'What do you mean?'

'We could get married,' he said. 'There's nothing to stop us.'

'Yes, there is,' she said almost peevishly, feeling she had sustained too many shocks and new ideas altogether within the last hour or so. 'There's Michael—and——' she raised an agitated hand to her forehead, '—and the fact that we don't love each other—at least, not in the right way——'

'What is the right way?' he queried, sounding amused.

'Oh, you know what I mean!' she told him crossly.

'All right, I do,' he conceded. 'You know, people get married for all sorts of reasons, not always because they've fallen madly in love.'

'Maybe,' she said, 'but I've always thought—after all, you were madly in love with Jill, weren't you?'

'Yes,' he said simply.

Dimly she began to see. That kind of love was a once-in-a-lifetime experience, and he didn't expect to find it again with anyone else. No doubt he was lonely, though, and he would like to marry someone for more humdrum reasons—companionship, a mother for Benjy, regular sex . . .

And what about her? She had thought Michael was the love of her life, but Michael was going to marry Francine. Where did that leave her? If it only happened once, was she going to spend the rest of her life alone, mourning her lost and wasted youth?

She shook her head; she couldn't marry

Simon just because it was *convenient* to do so. And he couldn't marry her, either, for that reason. Could he? She looked up into his face, trying to fathom his expression. His eyes were warm and questioning, and somehow his steady gaze flustered her. Uncertainly, she said, 'It's a crazy idea.'

'I don't think so.' He was quite imperturbable.

'It is!' she insisted. 'Anyway, I can't even think about it now! I've had enough for one day . . .'

'Yes, of course,' he said, and kissed her brow. 'I'm sorry, forget it for now, okay? Just leave things to me. I'll phone Anneke tonight, if you like, after she comes off duty, and break the news. Then all you need to do is accept her congratulations in the morning.'

'Oh, thank you, Simon,' she said, almost in tears. 'Thank you so much, for everything.'

'Don't say that!' he said, his deep, beautiful voice almost rough. 'Just think about what I said, later when you can do it quietly and calmly. It will work out all right, Meredith, I promise you.'

It didn't occur to her until hours afterwards to wonder how on earth he thought that could happen; he sounded so confident all she could do was lean her forehead gratefully against the shoulder of his blue shirt and say in muffled tones, 'I don't know why you're being so kind to me.'

'I told you,' he said, 'I have an ulterior motive.' His hand moved to her back, drawing her closer. She felt the warmth of his long, lean body, the muscularity of it, and to her utter surprise she recognised a sexual quality to the embrace, not just on his part, but on hers, too.

She lifted her head, astonished, and he smiled down into her eyes and said, 'Your parents will be expecting you to kiss me goodbye.'

Before she could answer, his mouth descended on hers, very firmly, and she found herself responding almost as she had earlier, even though this time she knew it was Simon, not Michael. And the sensations she felt were just the same. It was very peculiar . . .

His lips parted hers gently and she let him do that, and more; she would have let him do anything—anything at all.

When he drew back, his eyes had gone dark, the pupils huge. He smiled at her, and she stared back, utterly bemused. He let her go very slowly, and said, 'Give it some thought, Meredith.'

She swallowed and nodded, quite beyond speech. She wasn't even sure what it was she was supposed to give some thought to. That kiss? Or the fantastic suggestion that they could get married and give credence to the engagement that he had invented on the spur of the moment?

CHAPTER THREE

HER mother came into her room as she was getting into bed that night. 'You've quite recovered from your touch of the sun, haven't you?' she asked.

Meredith reassured her on that point, but she still lingered. 'Merrie, darling, naturally we're pleased with your news, but—well, I can't help feeling a bit surprised. Of course, you've spent a lot of time at the Van Dyks, and you know Simon well, but you've never even been out on a date with him. I must admit, I thought it was Michael you were interested in. I wondered if—Did you know that Michael was engaged before today?'

'No. I had no idea until I came into the room this afternoon and saw him—with Francine.'

She cast around for a way to explain the absurd situation she found herself in, but her mother had sat on the bed with a sigh of relief, her face clearing into a smile. 'Well, that's all right, then. I'm sorry, darling, it's just that the thought crossed my mind you might have heard from Michael that he'd found someone else, and accepted Simon's proposal on the rebound, so to speak.'

'No, it wasn't at all like that——'

'Good. I suppose it was silly of me to think so. You know we're fond of Michael, I would have been quite happy for you to marry him if your feelings hadn't changed. But it was only puppy love, after all, wasn't it?'

'I suppose so,' Meredith said slowly. It must have been that on his part, anyway. For Michael, it hadn't lasted.

'Well, Jean always said so, and I suppose she knows her son, though I wasn't sure about you. I think Simon will make you a much better husband, you know.'

'Do you?' Meredith was surprised. 'Why?'

Her mother laughed. 'You may not realise it, but you're a very strong-minded young woman. I've watched you with Michael, and he was quite willing to have you organise things for him. I was afraid it might not be good for you.'

'You mean I'm bossy?'

'No, not really. But you could be if you married a man who let you walk all over him.'

'Michael wouldn't . . . '

'I'm not so sure. Michael likes a quiet life. He doesn't mind at all having other people arrange it for him. His uncle arranged his career, and a place in the firm for him, and you were—I thought—arranging his marriage. It might have suited you, too, being the type of wife who pushes her husband up the ladder to success. But somehow I don't think it's really what you want. I'd like to see you marry a man who can match your strength of character.'

'And you think Simon would keep me in my place, do you?'

'That isn't what I meant at all. Simon's more mature, and he won't let anyone push him around.'

'I never pushed Michael around!'

'Are you sure?' her mother asked shrewdly. 'You certainly used to do it when you were both children, and I think the habit stuck a little. You just got a bit more tactful about it, that's all.'

There might be some truth in that, Meredith supposed reluctantly. Certainly Michael had nearly always fallen in with her plans, and if they had an argument he generally admitted she was right in the end, and gave in. He was an easygoing person, even as a child. She couldn't remember him ever really losing his temper. He didn't like people being angry with him, and if he was annoyed, himself, he was likely to go off on his own and sulk for a while, rather than start a fight. Later he would come back and go on as if nothing had happened. Meredith, who as a child had had to learn to control a naturally fierce temper, thought him a much nicer person than herself, and as she grew old enough to fall in love, had worked hard to avoid hurting Michael with her more outspoken nature.

'Anyway,' her mother was saying briskly, 'I'll let you go to sleep. But I *am* glad about you and Simon. I couldn't wish for a better son-in-law, and I'm sure you'll both be very happy.' She dropped a kiss on Meredith's cheek and stood up. 'Good night.'

'Good night,' Meredith echoed. She had meant to confide in her mother, but somehow the moment had passed. Just as well, perhaps. Evelyn Townsend was as honest as the day. Confronted with a deception, her natural impulse would be to advise Meredith to confess it and take the consequences. And Meredith couldn't help but be infinitely glad that no one except, unavoidably, Simon, was aware of the hurt she had suffered. If she told people now that Simon had only pretended to be engaged to her, her humiliation would be even worse than it would have been without his 'rescue' act. No one could fail to deduce that she had been expecting Michael to propose to herself, when he had turned up at her home with the girl he was going to marry. Her short-lived 'engagement' would be seen for exactly what it was, a charade invented to save face.

Meeting Anneke when she bowled into Meredith's small office at lunch time, her blonde curls bouncing and her eyes alight with curiosity and excitement, was not as bad as Meredith had feared. 'You dark horse!' Anneke accused her. 'When Simon told me I nearly dropped! You might have given me a teeny little hint or two. Dragging Michael in front of me all these years as a red herring, too!'

'Oh, not really,' Meredith protested feebly. 'It hasn't been years—we only realised quite recently——'

'Simon might have, but I suspect you've been nursing a secret passion. I remember you had a bit of a yen for him when we were in the third form, but I thought you'd got over that!'

'So did I,' Meredith said, feeling her way and trying to say as little possible. It wasn't difficult, really, excitement made Anneke talkative. Simon must have been pretty clever, because he seemed to have given his sister the impression that he and Meredith had gradually grown close over the past several months at least, but hadn't wanted to give their families any cause for speculation, so had cautiously kept it quiet until finally he had proposed and been accepted. It must have sounded very logical and reasonable, because Anneke now claimed to remember all kinds of incidents that might have given her a clue if only she had taken notice at the time. 'Of course, you've always got on terribly well,' she said knowledgeably. 'Though even when you were only a bit of a teenager you argued with him, didn't you?'

'He enjoyed it,' Meredith interjected.

'Yes, I know. Simon always loved a good

argument. My father says he gets it from his grandfather in the Netherlands. He says Opa would argue that black was white until his opponent gave up and agreed with him, and then he'd turn round and say, 'But on the other hand, it's possible that it's not so . . . ' and he'd start arguing the opposite point of view. He called it stimulating discussion.'

'Simon called it sharpening my logical reflexes,' Meredith laughed. 'I think it started when I was on the fourth form debating team for that inter-house competition, remember? And he got interested and started coaching me whenever he was here.'

'Well, he was the leader of the team that won the Carnfield Cup for it when he was at school, you know. He was terribly proud of you when you won.'

'I know. He kissed my cheek. Well, he's your brother, but the other girls in 4B were green with envy. They all thought he was dishy!'

Anneke chuckled. 'Just as well Jill didn't mind!'

'Heavens, we were only schoolgirls! There wasn't anything to mind about. It was lovely of him to come up specially for the evening though.'

'I'm sorry, Meredith.' Anneke looked uncomfortable.

'What about?' Meredith asked blankly.

'Well, mentioning Jill like that. Tactless of me.'

'Of course not! You can't go about trying not to mention poor Jill every time you're near me. I loved her, too, you know. Everyone did. And I know Simon——' She stopped abruptly. Simon still loved Jill, could never love anyone else in the same way, but he was pretending to be in love with Meredith, pretending that he wanted her for his wife. Careful. 'Simon,' she said, 'won't want to forget her, even if he could. Only, life goes on,' she tacked on tritely. Shut up, she told herself. Discretion is the better part of deception. Let Anneke do the talking. She's good at it.

Simon phoned her before she left the office at five. 'Can I meet you in town?' he asked. 'We should talk.'

'Yes,' she agreed. They certainly should. And it would be better away from her home where there was no possibility of being either overheard or interrupted. 'I'll miss my bus, though.'

'I'll take you home afterwards, of course,' he said a trifle curtly. He lived in the city, himself, although he worked for the oil refinery south of Whangarei as an industrial chemist. The job he had taken there was a step down for him, but after Jill's death he had wanted his son brought up by his parents, not strangers, and had given up a very good position in Auckland so that he could be near his child, taking the first suitable vacancy that was offered in the region. Meredith knew that Mr and Mrs Van Dyk would have made room for him, but he had bought a small house in the city, loath to crowd his parents' home any more, and knowing, as he had once told Meredith, that grown children going back to the parental home didn't fit in. Whangarei was roughly half way between the Van Dyk farm and the refinery, so it was almost an ideal arrangement. Some weekends he worked, but the rest he spent with Benjy, usually at the farm, though occasionally the little boy would stay at his father's house overnight.

He met her outside her office and said,

'The car's parked around the corner. Would you like to go to a restaurant, or shall we buy something and take it to my place?'

'Your place,' she said instantly. It was more private, and above all, she felt, they needed privacy.

He bought pizza, chips and salad, and she held the steaming bags while he negotiated the rush-hour traffic and eventually turned into the quiet street, under the shadow of bush-covered hills that backdropped the city. She had always liked his house. It wasn't big, but it was interesting, built of natural wood, with tall narrow windows that let in lots of light. There were trees around it—rough-barked, skinny kanuka, ponga ferns with black, hairy trunks and silver-backed fronds of leaves, and a couple of young totaras. Although there were neighbours not far away, the effect was of isolation. At the front of the house there was very little garden, just a few huge grey stones with rockery plants and ornamental grasses allowed to grow wild, and at the back the section merged into the bush, but a small level lawn had been cleared, and Simon had built a sandpit and hung a swing from one of the trees at the edge of the grass for Benjy.

The kitchen had a big porthole window looking out on the lawn, and Meredith, as she placed the food on plates while Simon put away his briefcase and freshened up, stopped what she was doing to watch a cock pheasant stalk across the grass, his brilliant tail catching the late sun that slanted down the hillside and glanced over the tops of the dark, round-headed trees.

'Caught you shirking, have I?' Simon said as he walked into the room. He came up behind her and she stiffened as his hands went to her waist, pulling her back against him. He had rolled up the sleeves of his white shirt, and she could feel the warmth of his arms through her thin summer dress.

'I was watching the pheasant,' she said, her voice muffled by a sudden constriction in her throat.

'He's a beauty, isn't he?' His breath stirred her hair at the temples, the fine little strands that escaped the thick, heavy chignon she wore for work. She felt the slight abrasiveness of his chin and caught a whiff of faint, spicy perfume. Had he been putting aftershave on for her benefit? The pheasant stretched his wings, ruffled his feathers and scuttled abruptly for the shelter of the trees. Simon released his hold and said, 'Let's have some wine. White or red?'

'White,' she answered, relieved that he was moving away. She had known Simon forever and he had never had this effect on her before, even when his picture had joined the pop stars and TV actors that had for a short period adorned the walls of her bedroom. Well, of course he hadn't kissed her then, she was only a child . . .

She was a child no longer, and he had no trouble tacitly reminding her of the fact. She wondered if he did it on purpose.

They ate at the small table in a corner of the kitchen, sitting on plain wooden chairs softened by flat gingham cushions.

'Did you tell your mother you'd be late?' Simon asked her.

'Yes, of course. She said as long as I was with you she wouldn't worry.'

'Is that a hint?'

She looked at him uncomprehendingly. 'About what?'

A disconcerting expression appeared in his eyes. The silence stretched, and then he shrugged and said, 'Never mind.' He poured some wine into the glass in front of her and said, 'Try that.'

It was a light and sparkling, and after having two glasses of it with the pizza, Meredith felt more relaxed.

Simon picked up the bottle and offered silently to refill her glass as she pushed away her plate, but she shook her head.

'Wise girl,' he commented, but he half filled his own glass and sipped it while she stood up and took the empty plates to the sink. As she rinsed them she glanced out of the window and saw two small black rabbits emerge from the edge of the bush, scampering across the short grass in a game of chase.

'Oh, look!' she said delightedly, and Simon got up, holding his glass, and came to stand beside her, his arm going round her shoulder.

'Cute little beggars, aren't they?' he said. 'My father wouldn't think so, of course.'

'No, he'd be reaching for his gun,' she agreed. 'I know farmers can't afford to be sentimental about noxious animals, but aren't they pretty?'

They watched while the rabbits played about, occasionally stopping to nibble at some blades of grass, and finally loping off again into the thick growth of ferns under the trees. Then Meredith, becoming aware of the light weight of Simon's arm across her shoulders, stirred. But instead of dropping his hand, he put his glass down on the bench in front of them and tightened his grip, bringing her into the circle of his arm, and pushing up her chin with his other hand.

Meredith drew in a sharp breath, her eyes widening before they closed as his lips came down on hers, firm, warm and compelling. His hands slid from her chin to her throat and lingered there, the thumb caressing her skin, and then his long fingers curved around her nape, lightly supporting her head. Meredith's hands were on his sleeves, feeling through the cloth the taut muscles of his upper arms. She resisted a strong desire to caress them, and instead tentatively pushed against him.

He didn't let her go straight away, but after a moment or two his grip relaxed and his mouth left hers. She stepped away from him, saying breathlessly, 'Please don't—we shouldn't!'

He laughed down at her flushed face. 'Why

ever not?'

Turning away and clutching the edge of the bench with one hand, she put the other to her temples for a moment and silently shook her head, trying to formulate a sensible speech from the incoherence of her thoughts.

Simon touched her arm, coaxingly running his fingers from her elbow to the sleeve of her dress. 'We are engaged, after all. Engaged couples generally kiss each other, don't they?'

'But we're not!' she said vehemently, swinging round to face him. 'Not really.'

'I'll buy you a ring,' he offered, smiling. 'Will that make it real?'

'Oh, *Simon*!' she snapped, just resisting the desire to stamp her foot with temper. 'Will you be serious!'

'I am,' he said. Then, looking at her stormy face, he stopped smiling and said soothingly, 'Shh.' He took her hands in his and began walking backwards, tugging her with him from the kitchen into the living room, talking all the time. 'All right, Meredith darling, let's be serious. Come on, we'll sit down and talk about it properly.'

'The dishes,' she said feebly as he pulled her through the doorway.

His smile flashed again briefly. 'Never mind the dishes. I'll do them later.' They were on the faded cotton rug in the centre of the polished floor, and when they reached the low, cushioned sofa, he sat down, bringing her with him, his hands still holding hers, so that they were half facing each other.

'Now,' he said, 'what's the trouble?'

'You know what the trouble is! We can't go on pretending to be engaged. It's—it's ridiculous!'

'You didn't think so yesterday. In fact you said more than once that you were grateful for it.'

'I know, but——' She looked away from him, biting her lip.

'And we needn't go on pretending,' he said. 'I offered a solution, remember? Have you thought about it?'

Her hands moved agitatedly in his, and he released them. She said, 'That's even crazier then a pretended engagement. You don't really want to marry me.'

'On the contrary, I would like very much to marry you,' he argued. 'I thought I'd made that clear.'

She shot him a look compounded of

curiosity and incredulity. 'I don't understand.'

His answering look was impatient. 'Don't
be silly, Meredith,' he said shortly. 'Of course
you understand. You're not a baby.'

Her cheeks flamed. It was so unusual for
him to lose patience that she felt herself
inwardly trembling. She looked down at her
hands, twisting them together. 'It's just——'
she said in a low voice, '—I'm not accustomed to thinking of you in that way.'

'Aren't you?' His voice was dry. 'It seems
to me that it wouldn't be too hard for you
to become accustomed to it. Each time I've
kissed you in the last two days you've
responded very nicely.'

'The first time doesn't count.'

'All right, the first time doesn't count,' he
agreed evenly. He seemed to have recovered
his equilibrium. 'You thought I was Michael.
But the next time—and just now in the
kitchen—you were kissing *me*. Weren't you?'

She hunched a shoulder, embarrassed by
his frank question, unwilling to admit that in
spite of her feelings for Michael she could so
easily be aroused by another man. 'Maybe,'
she muttered.

His voice sharpened. *'Maybe?'* His hand came up, the long fingers cupping her face and making her look at him. The accusing anger in his eyes shocked her and her heart skipped with alarm. 'Did you close your eyes and think of Michael, or *were you kissing me*?'

'Simon——'

He said softly, 'Answer me, Meredith, honestly.'

She parted her lips and moistened them with her tongue, her gaze held inescapably by his hard blue stare. 'You,' she whispered.

His expression altered only slightly. Satisfaction briefly lifted the corners of his mouth. 'So,' he said, 'let's have no more nonsense about how you think of me. You're a woman, and you think of me as a man. I'm not your big brother.'

That was the problem, of course. He was Anneke's big brother, and in all the years she had known him he had treated her exactly like another little sister, until yesterday. The sudden shift in their relationship had left her floundering in unknown seas. 'It takes some getting used to,' she said.

He released her chin and put his hand over

both hers where they lay in her lap. 'Yes, I suppose it does,' he conceded. 'But there's no going back, Meredith.'

She knew what he meant. Part of her wanted to return to the easy, uncomplicated friendship they had shared when he was a young man and she was a little girl. She supposed that since adolescence she had been conscious of him as a personable male, but after that first stirring of sexuality which she had virtually sublimated into hero-worship, she had suppressed all those feelings for him. He was a married man and much too old for her, anyway. Michael had made a more suitable, attainable and less dangerous object for her affections. Now Michael no longer stood between them, and at thirty-one Simon was hardly too old for her twenty-two.

There were other complications, though. Michael might have decided to marry someone else, but that didn't alter the way she felt about him. The trauma of finding herself supposedly engaged to Simon, and the turmoil of mind that it engendered, had pushed conscious thoughts of Michael to the background of her mind, but last night after her mother left her she had eventually cried herself to sleep, cursing her own weakness all the while, and throughout today she had carried within her a sort of hard, persistent lump of unhappiness.

Her mouth drooped suddenly, and she badly wanted to cry again. Turning her head away, she blinked rapidly to dispel the threat of tears. Simon made a soft little sound and took her in his arms, pushing her head against his shoulder. 'It's all right, little one,' he said. 'We'll work it out, don't you worry.'

For a moment she had the absurd feeling of being a child again, confiding her troubles to Simon who would make them come right. His fingers stroked her cheek and hair, and she sniffed and said, 'Work what out?' He couldn't bring Michael back to her, and that was really all she wanted, wasn't it?

'Everything.' He sounded so confident that she giggled.

A smile in his voice, he said, 'What's so funny?'

'You. Superhero, aren't you?' She deepened her voice to imitate a masculine intonation. 'Don't you worry your pretty little head, Scarlett honey. I'll fix everything.'

His laughter shook his chest, and she lifted

her head to look at him. He really looked very good at close quarters. His skin tanned lightly in the summer, and with his fair hair and even white teeth, not to mention the blue vividness of his eyes, it made him extremely attractive. Her gaze involuntarily went from his face to the unbuttoned neck of his shirt, and she was suddenly conscious of their closeness, of his thigh against hers, his hand on her waist, her own hands flat on the material of his shirt, not far from the tantalising opening at his throat. His eyes narrowed suddenly, and his fingers tightened their hold on her waist. She took a quick breath, avoiding his eyes, and tried to move away.

'Don't fight it,' he said. 'There's no need.'

Breathlessly she said, 'I love Michael.'

'Michael doesn't want you.'

She raised hurt eyes to his face, amazed at his cruelty, and caught a blue glitter in his eyes before he pulled her quite roughly towards him and kissed her with more passion than gentleness, pressing her head against the back of the sofa and forcing her mouth open beneath his. One hand went from her waist to her midriff and then firmly cupped her breast, and her heart gave a bound and then settled into a faster rhythm.

He lifted his mouth and looked down at where he was touching her, and then back to her face. Deliberately he said, 'I, on the other hand, want you very much.'

She tried to say that she didn't want him, but he was caressing her breast, finding with his thumb and forefinger the physical reaction that belied her. Confused and embarrassed, she turned her head, hiding her face against his shirt, her forehead resting on the warm flesh at the base of his throat.

His hand came up to stroke her face, and she felt his lips on her temple, smoothing over the agitated pulse-beat. 'You can't deny that you want me, too,' he said quietly.

She shook her head. 'It isn't the same thing.'

His caressing hand stopped for a moment. 'No,' he conceded, 'it isn't. But it's good enough for me—meantime.'

His hand lightly stroked her neck and then began moving on her shoulder. It was very soothing, and she had an urge to purr. She also felt drowsy, and the lump of unhappiness that had lain like lead in her chest all day had almost dissipated.

He said, 'I asked you to think about marrying me. You've only to say the word, and our engagement will be as real as anyone else's.'

She stirred agitatedly, and he dropped a quick kiss on her cheek as though it would restrain her. 'Michael has Francine,' he reminded her ruthlessly, though his voice was low and gentle. 'I know you think your heart is broken. Perhaps it isn't much use telling you that you'll get over it. But I'm sure you will. Heartbreak doesn't last for ever. Even the worst.'

'You mean—Jill?'

'Yes. In the early days after it happened I thought I'd never recover, it was like dying myself, I had no feelings left but grief. But now I can think of her in the happy times, see her in Benjamin sometimes, and feel glad—glad that we shared so much, glad that I knew her and loved her, that I can see her smile, her love of music, her sense of humour, in our son. That's a compensation. The memories aren't often painful now.'

He had so much more to grieve over than she did, Meredith felt ashamed. Michael might prefer another woman over her, but at least he was alive. And so was she. Like Simon, some day she would learn to live again without pain. Only at the moment that day seemed a long way off.

Simon understood. He had been through infinitely worse than what she was experiencing. And he wouldn't expect too much. He, too, had another love in his past. He was suggesting a sensible solution for both of them. Because he had problems, too. She said, 'You must have been lonely since she died.'

'Yes, at first unbearably so, in spite of having Ben and my family—and yours.'

'There must have been other girls—women—you might have married, though.'

'I suppose so. At first I was too shattered to think of it. Then I did—think of it—for Ben's sake. Only it didn't seem fair.'

'To——?'

'To the women. Woman. I found I couldn't cast around coldbloodedly for a stepmother for my son. If she was fond of me, I'd be cheating her.'

Because he couldn't feel for any other woman the love he had felt for Jill, she knew. But she was different, of course. Simon could be confident she had no illusions because she had known him and Jill when they were young and in love, and she would not expect him to be able to love her in that way. The thought created an unexpected feeling of depression, and as though sensing it he said, his mouth moving against her hair, 'I love you, Meredith. Will you marry me?'

Of course he loved her, she knew that—as he loved Anneke and Benjy, with the added fillip of sexual attraction in her case because she had grown from the child he had been fond of into a nubile young woman. If she wasn't as beautiful as Jill had been, she was reasonably nice looking. She loved him, too, but not in the way she had loved Michael, and she found the new element of sex that Simon had introduced into their relationship somewhat bewildering.

There was no doubt that she was sexually responsive to him. Perhaps it was possible to be like that with any man. She had very little experience with anyone but Michael. It was disconcerting to find that Simon could exact from her equally, if not more, passionate reactions. He was older, of course, and had been married, and she supposed—although

the thought filled her with sudden distaste—
he might have had affairs since. Four years
of celibate windowhood sounded unlikely,
after all. Still, she knew he wasn't the type to
be promiscuous. No wonder he wanted to get
married again, even without the first fine
careless rapture of youthful love.

Tenderness and an aching sorrow flooded
her with a suddenness that was startling.
Simon deserved a loving wife, and a proper
home and family life. His own parents had
such a warm, happy and protective atmosphere in their home, he must miss it
dreadfully. His house was attractive, but
seemed strangely unlived in. The furniture
was good, most of it chosen by him and Jill
together when they were first married, and
there were even pictures on the walls and
ornaments on the mantel over the brass-
hooded fireplace. But, perhaps because Simon
spent most of his leisure time at the farm, the
air of emptiness about the house was
palpable, in spite of the efforts of his mother
and sisters to provide extra comforts like
embroidered cushions and hand-made rugs.
They only cluttered the rooms without really
warming them. It was a lovely house still

waiting to be made into a home, rather than just a place to eat and sleep.

She could do that for him. Suddenly she wanted very much to do it. She had, after all, planned exactly that for Michael. But he didn't need her. Simon needed her. He had said yesterday that he had an ulterior motive. And what better use could she find for her life since Michael turned his back on her love? She certainly didn't want to go through life wishing for what might have been. And supposing she did get over Michael and fall in love again? She didn't really want to experience that cycle of love-happiness-betrayal again. Once was quite enough. Maybe being madly in love wasn't such a great basis for marriage, anyway. Her own pioneer great-grandmother had married a man she scarcely knew, seemingly because he was the only single man around of the right age and 'sober habits', and her diary showed no subsequent regrets.

'Meredith?' Simon's voice was low in her ear, barely more than a whisper. 'Is it such a difficult decision?'

'Yes,' she said.

'Yes, it is, or Yes, you'll marry me?'

She took a deep breath. 'Yes, I'll marry you, Simon.'

CHAPTER FOUR

ON the following Friday night they bought a ring, the traditional solitaire diamond in a simple gold setting. Jill, Meredith remembered, had worn a sapphire cluster. She pushed the thought from her mind as Simon scrawled his signature on the cheque and picked up the small parcel from the counter.

He turned to her with a smile and led her out of the shop. 'Let's find somewhere quiet,' he suggested.

They went back to his car, and he drove towards her home, but stopped on the way in a small layby overlooking tranquil Northland hills with pockets of bush tucked into hollows between green, sheep-dappled paddocks. The light was fading, and two or three stars, dimly glittering, pricked the faded canopy of the sky.

Simon wound down his window and took the wrapped box from his pocket. Meredith found herself strangely nervous as she watched him pull off the little strip of Sellotape and discard the square of paper in the ashtray under the dashboard. He looked up and smiled at her as he flipped up the lid of the red leather box, and she tried to smile back.

'Give me your hand,' he said.

Slowly he slid the gold band with its glittering focus on to the third finger. She felt herself tremble, and his hold tightened. Then he bent his head and kissed her knuckle just above the ring.

Convulsively, she clutched his hand, and he looked up into her eyes. 'You look scared stiff,' he said. 'There's nothing to be frightened of.'

'I know. I'm not scared. It's just—nerves.'

'Bridal nerves already?' He drew her into his arms, kissing the top of her head. 'A bit early, isn't it?' They had planned the wedding for the new year, and this was barely December.

'Sorry,' she murmured. 'I've never got officially engaged before.'

'There's a first time for everything.' It wasn't his first time, of course. She wondered if he had given Jill her ring in just the same way, kissed her hand afterwards . . .

Trying to blot out thoughts of Jill, odious

comparisons, she moved restlessly. Perhaps he misinterpreted her action, which brought her breasts into closer contact with his chest. His arm about her tightened, and his mouth wandered from her hair to her temple and down her cheek, while his free hand lifted her face to allow him to find her mouth.

The kiss was exceedingly gentle, and she was touched because she thought he was being careful not to make her 'bridal nerves' worse.

When he drew away she was mildly disappointed, and had to stop herself from pulling down his head again and offering her eagerly parted lips.

He sat with his hand on her nape, caressing the smooth skin under the fall of her long hair. Meredith looked down to hide the look in her eyes. 'All right?' he enquired.

She nodded, and he said, 'We'd better get on. The families will want to see the ring.'

'Have you explained to Benjy?' she asked him as he started the car.

'Yes. I doubt if he fully understands, but he has grasped the point that you're going to be living with me in my house, and that eventually he'll be with us permanently.'

'Eventually?'

'I thought we'd have some time on our own first. Give you a chance to get used to being married before foisting a stepson on to you.'

'You're not foisting Benjy on me! I'm looking forward to being his——'

'His mother. He doesn't remember Jill, you know. You'll be to all intents and purposes his mother.'

'*Your* mother has been that. She's going to miss him.'

'Yes, she will. Another reason why it seems better all round to make the transition gradually. She's been wonderful, of course, but it's asking a lot of a woman who's already brought up a family of her own to take on another baby.'

'I'm sure she didn't mind. And Christopher was only six years older. I'm often amused at the way Benjy calls him "Uncle".'

'That was my idea. I didn't want him to get confused about exactly who he is. My son, although his grandparents have taken on the parenting of him. And Chris's nephew, not his brother. In a big family like ours, relationships are complicated enough without adding to the problem of sorting them out. Ben has had to get used to several cousins already, as well as his aunts and uncles. My mother had just emerged from twenty-six years of looking after small children. Offering to have Benjamin was almost heroic, in the circumstances. I shouldn't really have let her, but at the same time I was so shattered I couldn't think what to do except gratefully accept. And then, when I realised, it was too late. I didn't want to unsettle him, and my mother wouldn't hear of my getting a house-keeper to care for him.'

'He's a lovely little boy.'

He cast her an amused glance. 'He can be a little terror, you know. You may not think he's so lovely when you have to cope with him on your own.'

On her mettle, she said, 'We'll be all right. We've always got on fine. And I see what you mean about making the transition gradually, but you really don't need to delay having him to live with you on my account, Simon.'

'Maybe it isn't only on your account.'

'What do you mean?'

'Hasn't it occurred to you that I might just want you to myself for a while?'

He gave her a sideways glance that made her blush fiercely and kept her speechless for the next ten minutes, by which time they had arrived at the gateway of her home.

Her parents duly admired the ring, and then they took torches and in the balmy night air, pungent with the scents of cow-dung and milking sheds, walked over to the Van Dyks'. Simon's father handed round drinks and the evening soon turned into a convivial family celebration. At ten o'clock, while Anneke, home for the weekend, and her teenage sister Josie played a duet on guitar and recorder, Meredith looked at Benjy, asleep on his father's knee, and felt a quite extraordinary surge of tenderness. She had always been fond of Benjy, but now, knowing that she was going to accept the responsibility of a parent, her feelings had become stronger than that. Simon caught her eye and smiled, then looked down at the sleeping boy and stood up, saying to his mother, 'I'll put him to bed.'

'Can I come?' Meredith asked.

'Of course.' He waited for her, and Meredith got up to join him, preceding him out into the short passageway that led to the room Benjy and Christopher shared. Glancing back, she saw Mrs Van Dyk smiling approval, though there was a strained look about the smile. It would be hard for her to part with Benjy, but Whangarei wasn't far away, and even if he wasn't living in their house any more, he would still see his grandparents often. She and Simon would make sure of that.

She found the light switch and pulled back the bedclothes. Simon bent to lay the sleeping child down, watching while she tucked in the single blanket and sheet. She kissed Benjy's cheek and turned to see Simon watching her intently. A little disconcerted, she pushed back a wayward strand of hair with a jerky movement, looking at him with something like apprehension. He stretched out a hand to switch off the light, and as she made to pass him in the doorway his arm swept across in front of her and pulled her to him. In the darkness he found her mouth and kissed her with a kind of fierceness, bending her back against his arm.

She was off balance, clutching at his shoulders, her heart thudding with nervous excitement. She made a protesting, negative movement, and he let her go so quickly that she stumbled against the door jamb, trying to stay on her feet. His hand shot out to steady her, his fingers closing on her arm. 'Are you all right?' he asked her, his voice sounding rough-edged although he kept it low.

'Yes,' she said. 'But next time you might give me some warning.'

'Sorry.' He released her arm and fleetingly ran his hand down her cheek. 'I'll try to keep my carnal impulses under control in future.'

Would that apply when they were married? She supposed not. If anyone had asked her a month ago, she would have hazarded a guess that Simon would be the very gentlest of lovers. But since that day when he had first kissed her, she had discovered a new person underneath the smooth, calm surface of his character. Sometimes he seemed to be a slightly alarming stranger.

In the lounge the conversation had drifted to romance and lovers' meetings. Mrs Van Dyk, in her rich Netherlands accent, was telling the story of how she came to New Zealand to marry the man who had left their small village two years before, promising to send for her when he had a job, some money and the prospect of a home. He had been working in a dairy factory on the Wairarapa, and she had arrived by train. 'I saw him as the train passed, looking for me, but he couldn't see me, and when the train stopped, there he was at the other end of the platform. I got out and dropped my case, and yelled, "Frans! *Ik ben hier, kaaskop!*" And he turned around and started to run. Then I started running too, and there we were racing down that long platform to each other, with all the Kiwis staring at us as if we were mad. Crazy Dutchies, we were. But not seeing each other for two years! And we were young, and in love.' She laughed, wiping her eyes, and exchanged a fond look with her husband of thirty-two years.

Everyone has heard the story before, but they all laughed. Maria's family had thought she was mad, too, travelling half way round the world to marry her Frans, but she had been very happy with him. Meredith had often heard her tell stories of the hard times when money had been short and the children were small and demanding, 'But,' she would say, shrugging and laughing, 'we were young, and we loved each other. We got by.'

Mrs Van Dyk was a great believer in romantic love. No doubt she thought that Simon had fallen in love again. When the Townsends got up to go, she shooed Simon out the door with them, pressing a torch into his hand and saying, 'Go on, walk your fiancée home.'

His car was still at the Townsends, anyway. He brought Meredith to a half when they reached it, with his hand on her wrist, letting her parents go on into the house. He switched off the torch and dropped it through the open window of the car on to the soft leather of the seat. 'I'm giving you fair warning this time,' he said. 'I'm about to kiss you good night.'

He drew her very slowly into his arms and kissed her forehead, her temples, her cheek, then softly touched her lips with his. His hand slid up her back, shaped her shoulder, and ran down her bare arm and up again, then came to rest on her breast. Her lips beneath parted involuntarily, and his kiss firmed and deepened, his other hand going lower on her back, holding her against his body. She gasped, the sound muffled in his mouth, and he broke the kiss, still holding her, trying to look into her eyes, but she hid her face against his shoulder. 'Do I frighten you?' he asked her.

She shook her head, but still wouldn't look at him. 'Meredith . . . ' He seemed about to ask her something else but changed his mind. Instead he eased her away from him and said, 'Will I see you tomorrow?'

'If you like. I'll be here.'

'Of course I like. I like you very much, Meredith, apart from—everything else.'

Everything else, she supposed, meant this breathless, heated feeling of frustrated desire. Did he feel it too? Well, obviously. Or something very like it, anyway. 'I like you, too,' she said, sounding like a polite little girl. She wasn't surprised to hear him laugh softly before he turned and got into the car. 'Good night, darling,' he said, and shut the door. She stepped back while he put the car into gear, and lifted her hand as he started the engine and turned towards the gate.

Several times the next day she sensed that he was about to ask her something, but he never did. They spent most of the time with Benjy, and in the afternoon they took him and Chris to the beach, arriving back at the farm with the two boys covered in sand and sunburn, just in time for the evening meal, which the Dutch immigrants had learned to call 'tea' like the native New Zealanders, instead of dinner or supper as they had been taught in their English classes back home. Mr Van Dyk had a favourite story about arriving in his new country and travelling for many hours after being given a cup of tea and a biscuit, always answering the well-meant query, 'Have you had tea?' with a polite, 'Yes, I have had some tea, thank you,' and never realising that he was being offered the meal that his empty stomach craved.

'Would you like to go out somewhere?' Simon asked her as they washed up the dishes together.

'Not tonight, I'm bushed.'

He grinned. 'Next week, then. I'll take you out dining and dancing on Saturday night,' he promised. 'We've never actually had a date, have we?'

'That's what my mother said.'

He looked at her enquiringly.

'That we'd never had a date,' she amplified. 'Well, it was a bit of a surprise to her, our engagement.'

'Yes, I suppose it was. We must make up for it, then. We'll paint the town before the wedding.'

He sent her flowers on Saturday, extravagantly, a bouquet of red roses in a box. She put them in a vase and broke the head off one to pin on to the low front of the white georgette blouse she wore with a black grosgrain skirt that evening. She had been going to wear black patent pumps, but at the last minute decided to change them for a pair of very high-heeled red sandals that matched the rose.

Simon approved her appearance with a glance, his gaze lingering on the rose resting in the shadowed hollow of her breasts. Then he smiled and held out his hand, leading her to his car and opening the door for her almost ceremonially.

She said, as he started the car, 'Thank you for the flowers.'

'Thank you for wearing one of them,' he answered. 'You look beautiful, and rather exotic. Like a gypsy queen.'

She laughed, because there was nothing exotic about her. She was a very ordinary girl, and she thought wistfully, briefly, of Jill's blonde loveliness. 'You look pretty good, yourself,' she complimented him. He was wearing a pleated shirt and bow tie with a dark suit, and she wished it didn't remind her of what he had worn on his wedding day.

Involuntarily, she said, 'Would you wear grey for our wedding?'

He cast her a look of some surprise. 'If that's what you want.'

It was, but she couldn't tell him why.

'Will you be wearing white?' he asked her.

'Of course.' She hesitated. 'Unless you'd rather I didn't.'

'Why should I?'

'Well, as it's not the first time for you . . .'

'But it is for you. Naturally you'll wear white. At least, I hoped that you would.'

'Well, my mother's taking it for granted. And so is yours,' she told him.

He smiled. 'Are they taking you over, Meredith? Shall we just quietly elope?'

'No, I don't mind. And I'm quite capable

of sticking up for myself if things get out of hand.'

'Yes, I think you are.'

Recalling her conversation with her mother the night that Simon had announced their 'engagement', she said, 'Mum thinks I'm inclined to rule the roost, but that you'll keep me in line.'

He glanced at her again, his eyes full of laughter. 'And what do you think?'

She remembered her realisation that day, too, that she wouldn't like to be on the wrong side of Simon. 'I think,' she said lightly, 'that we'll see about that.'

He laughed aloud. 'Yes, we will,' he said. 'It's going to be fun, isn't it?'

'Is it?' Her sideways look was a little wary.

His eyes glinted at her. 'Afraid?' he taunted gently.

'No.' But a shiver ran down her back, an emotion more complicated than fear, a strange excitement that contained fear as a minor element. Something she had never experienced before, but the kind of emotion she imagined that skydivers and racing drivers might feel, the attraction of living dangerously.

How odd that nice, familiar, safe Simon should arouse anything like that in her. She told herself she was being over imaginative; after all they had only been indulging in a little light badinage. But when he put out his hand and found hers, holding it firmly in his warm clasp, her heartbeats accelerated and the peculiar tension became so strong it constricted her throat.

At the restaurant she managed to relax a little as they ate and talked. On the dance floor later Simon held her closely. In all the years she had known him, they had never danced together before. He had a smooth, relaxed, rhythmic style, and she enjoyed herself tremendously. Their first date promised to be very successful.

She sighed with contentment, and he said, his lips moving against her temple, 'Tired?'

'No, happy,' she told him dreamily.

He lifted his head to look at her, a half-smile on his lips but his eyes sceptical. 'Are you?'

She remembered Michael then, realising with something of a shock that she had forgotten, this evening, to be unhappy; the familiar little ache that she had lately learned to live with had been absent. Almost defiantly, she said, 'Yes.'

'Well,' Simon said slowly, 'I'm glad.' But thinking of Michael had brought a shadow to her face and a shimmer of tears into her eyes. She wished he had not reminded her, and unreasonably blamed him for it. Abruptly she said, 'I'd like another drink. Let's sit down.'

They did, and he ordered some more of the sparkling white wine she had been drinking, and gradually she forgot her annoyance and her pain at Michael's defection, and began to sparkle herself.

Simon watched her with somewhat wary amusement, and when they finally left and in the cool night air she stumbled over her own feet going down the steps to the car park, he gripped her round the waist and said, his voice filled with laughter, 'My darling, I don't know what your parents will say. You're ever so slightly tipsy.'

'Don't care,' she said firmly. 'I feel great.'

'I'm glad to hear it. I wonder if you'll say that in the morning.'

'Oh, who cares about the morning? Let the morning take care of itself!' she said grandly, and slipped away from him as they reached the flat ground, to spread her arms wide in a theatrical gesture. Her high heels teetered, and Simon swooped and caught her into his arms before she fell. She laughed and flung her arms about his neck and said breathlessly, her eyes shining in the darkness, 'Kiss me, Simon.'

He did, gently at first and then less gently as her uninhibited response ignited him. A group of people coming down the steps whooping and whistling made them break apart, and she found herself almost hauled across the asphalt and thrust into Simon's car, the door slamming behind her. She blinked, slightly sobered, and as he slid in beside her enquired, 'Are you angry with me, Simon?'

He turned to look at her anxious face. 'No, of course not. Do up your seat belt. I'm taking you home.'

She fell asleep on the way, and he kissed her awake without passion, then deposited her on the doorstep, asking, 'Do you think you can make it to your room?'

'Of course I can,' she answered indignantly. 'I'm not drunk!'

'Not quite,' he said. 'Just delightfully irresponsible. Good night.' He kissed her nose, pushed the door open for her and went back to the car. It wasn't until she was taking off her blouse that she realised the rose was gone, and recalled the little tug with which he had deftly removed it before he went.

CHAPTER FIVE

MEREDITH had vetoed the idea of an engagement party, disappointing both her own mother and Simon's. One reason had been that she knew there would be no way to avoid inviting Michael and his family, and she didn't think that she could bear that.

She hadn't bargained on being asked to a party for Michael and Francine. Francine lived in Auckland, and Meredith had assumed any engagement celebrations would be held there, but apparently that wasn't good enough for Michael's family. They wanted to hold their own party for the engaged pair. And naturally the Townsends were on the guest list.

'I don't think I can go,' Meredith blurted out in a panic when her mother relayed the invitation. Catching the surprised look on Mrs Townsend's face, she improvised desperately, 'I think Simon has something arranged for that night. The refinery staff are having a social or something.'

'But I haven't told you the date yet!' her

mother protested, astonished.

Meredith flushed. 'Oh. Well, I assumed it was Saturday night . . . '

'Not this Saturday, next. And I don't think Simon can have anything arranged for that night. He told Katie and Jack he would look after the children for them while they go to a wedding down in Taupo that weekend, if they couldn't find anyone else. Katie rang her mother just this morning while I was over at the Van Dyk's, and mentioned they'd got a neighbour's daughter to stay the night, so Simon wouldn't be needed. Maria was going to phone him tonight to save Katie another toll call, and tell him he was off the hook.'

While Meredith was still casting about for a way out, her mother said, 'So that's all right, then. And of course Simon is included in the Kingsleys' invitation. You can both come.'

'Yes,' Meredith said, feeling trapped and clinging to the fact that at least Simon would be there to support her. 'I suppose we can.'

When she told him, Simon looked at her thoughtfully and said, 'Will you mind?'

'Yes,' she said tensely. 'I don't want to go. Can't we think of something . . . ? A prior engagement we forgot, or some important social function to do with your work?'

'I don't think so,' he said quietly. 'Do you?'

'No,' she sighed. 'I suppose not. They'd be hurt. Our families have been friends for ages.'

'Yes. And you can't avoid him forever. Especially if you don't want people to know how you felt about him.'

He was talking as if it was all in the past, but the past was very recent. The invitation had awakened the hurt again, so that she spent long periods before the party brooding over the good times that she and Michael had enjoyed together, the plans she had made, sometimes aloud. He had never demurred, had even seemed as happy as she to envisage a future together.

She went into the city with her parents on the night of the party, and they stopped to pick up Simon on the way. He sat next to Meredith in the back seat but talked mainly to her mother and father who were asking him questions over their shoulders, and he didn't touch Meredith. Her hands were clasped tightly together in her lap, and her back was rigid as they drew up outside the Kingsleys' home. There were a few cars there, and she was thankful to find the living room holding quite a crowd, making it easy for her to gloss over the brief meeting with Michael. Francine was clinging to her fiancé's arm and looking radiant. She was staying with the Kingsleys for the weekend, and they seemed already to be treating her as one of the family. She helped to pass around savouries and titbits, and joked easily with Michael's Uncle Barry who had always had an eye for a pretty girl.

The evening was hot, and the party spilled over on to the patio outside where someone set up a portable tape player, and the young people began to dance.

Meredith danced with Simon and some others that she knew, and was ready to sit out for a while when suddenly two hands grasped her waist from behind and she was swept back into the whirl of gyrating couples. She turned to find Michael grinning down at her, his handsome young face flushed with excitement and possibly drink, and as his arms closed loosely about her, she automatically matched her steps to his, their dancing so familiar to each other that she could follow his lead without even thinking about it. The music slowed, and more people were now dancing close instead of apart, the smallish space becoming crowded, so that, caught in the middle of the terrace, Michael and Meredith could do little more than sway in time to the music. Meredith closed her eyes, trying to pretend that nothing had changed, that it was still the two of them as it always had been, but a deep sadness inside her refused to go away, and she squeezed her lids tightly together to stop tears from escaping down her cheeks. She, too, had been drinking rather more than she was accustomed to, and this time it hadn't made her gay as on the night that Simon had taken her dancing, but rather induced a moody melancholy which had been deepening all evening.

Michael murmured, 'Just like old times, isn't it, Merrie?' and she nodded, a lump forming in her throat. The music stopped and some of the dancers wandered off the floor, but the tape was turned over and the slow tempo continued. Michael loosened his hold a little, and looked down at his partner. Meredith answered the unspoken question in his eyes with a silent consent, and his arms tightened again as they continued dancing.

Soon, however, the tune altered to a fast rock-and-roll number, and Michael said, 'Let's get out.'

He led her off the wooden terrace down a short flight of steps to the shadows of a spicy-scented pepper tree, his hand swinging hers as it had so often done before. 'Well,' he said, 'enjoying the party?'

It was such a banal question she almost laughed hysterically. 'Yes,' she lied. 'It's a lovely party. And Francine is a lovely girl,' she added, painfully sincere. 'You're very lucky.'

'I know.' He sounded both humble and just slightly smug, and Meredith's melancholy deepened alarmingly. Plaintively she said, 'You might have told me, don't you think?'

'Told you what?' His voice was guarded, and he let go of her hand so that it fell to her side.

'Well, that you were getting engaged. After all, we'd been—been close friends for an awfully long time.'

'Well, yes.' Now he was uncomfortable. 'But that's all, wasn't it? Just friends.'

Meredith drew in a quick, indignant breath,

and he said, 'After all, you wouldn't even let me—I mean, you can't count a few kisses in the holidays. It was hardly a serious love affair. We were just a couple of kids having a good time.'

Meredith was speechless. Did he mean that because she hadn't let him make love to her completely, he had thought her love was a shallow, meaningless thing? He hadn't seemed to mind too much at the time, although once or twice he had pressed her to go much further than she was willing to.

He thrust his hands into his pockets and said almost sulkily, 'Actually, I did mean to tell you first, but we got engaged rather suddenly, and there wasn't time to write. I thought I'd phone from home, when I could, but as soon as Mum heard the news she wanted to rush out to your place and tell your parents, and—well, there was no chance of making a private phone call. Anyway,' he added in injured tones, 'you weren't exactly waiting around for me, were you?'

But I *was*! she thought in anguish. I was doing exactly that! Only she couldn't say so now.

Michael put her thoughts into words. 'You

were busy getting engaged to Simon, yourself. You never told me you were seeing him. I don't see why you should be peeved about Francine and me.'

Stung, she said, 'I'm not peeved! I'm very pleased for you. I just thought you would have told me about it—earlier, that's all.'

'So why didn't you tell me about Simon?'

'That's different!'

'Why is it different?'

'Well, because—because I didn't get a chance. It only happened that afternoon.'

'Look, I told you,' he said exasperatedly. 'Francine and I only got engaged the day before we left Auckland. You're being a bit unreasonable, aren't you?'

'Unreasonable!' Her voice had risen. She didn't think it was at all unreasonable to have expected him to make an effort to break the news of his engagement to her before anyone else. And she was getting increasingly frustrated with the necessity to pretend a civilised indifference and to cancel from him that her engagement had not in fact preceded her knowledge of his. She wanted to fly at him with her fists or yell insults as she would have when they were both very young and

had quarrelled about something. A childish display of temper would have suited her mood very nicely.

A man was standing at the top of the steps. She saw his dark shape against the house lights and recognised Simon before he called her name: 'Meredith?'

Michael turned at the sound, and Meredith, with sudden urgency, brushed past him and almost ran up the steps. 'I was talking to Michael,' she said, breathless with emotion more than exertion. 'Were you looking for me?'

She couldn't see Simon's face clearly in the darkness, but he lifted his head as though seeking out Michael's shadowy figure under the tree. 'Just to see that you're all right,' he said. He looked down at her, and even in the dim light she thought his expression was searching. 'They're serving coffee inside,' he added prosaically. 'Would you like some?'

Unaccountably anxious, she grabbed at his arm. 'Yes, I would. What about you? Come on, let's go in.'

She stayed by him for the rest of the evening, not talking much but keeping away from the alcohol that was circulating. She had a feeling that it wouldn't take a great deal more to turn her into a maudlin drunk. Simon didn't drink a lot, either. She didn't remember ever seeing him take too much.

On the way home he held her hand until they reached his house, but she sensed that his thoughts were elsewhere. He seemed aloof, and she shivered in spite of the warm night. She would have liked to have his arm about her, to lean her head against his shoulder. A glance at his austere profile discouraged her, though. She wondered if he was annoyed that she had spent a few minutes with Michael in the garden. She couldn't ask him, with her parents in the car able to hear every word. Anyway, it was highly unlikely. He had no reason to mind, and he wasn't the jealous type. Besides, he didn't care for her strongly enough to be that way. When her father stopped the car, Simon brushed her lips quickly with his and got out with a brief thanks and good night for her parents.

Meredith and Simon had evening 'dates' alone, but at the weekends he still spent most of Saturday and Sunday with his son. Sometimes she refused his invitation to join them, thinking that Benjy might come to resent her if she always accompanied Simon. Better for him to get gradually used to the idea that they were a family threesome. On this particular Sunday, after Michael's party, she had been half expected at the Van Dyk's, she knew, but elected instead to stay at home. She cut out and started sewing a new dress that she had bought the material and pattern for that week. She had woken feeling depressed, and she had always found dressmaking a good palliative for that. Doing something creative was a pleasant, relaxing variation from the pragmatic, businesslike approach necessary in her job. She had tried painting but had not been good at it, had attended pottery lessons for a term and found them boring, though she admired the work and enthusiasm of others in the class. But she liked sewing, and making her own clothes satisfied the urge to do something useful and decorative with her hands.

Simon might welcome the time alone with his son. Also she thought there had been something of a chill in the air between Simon and herself last night. If he and Benjy really wanted her company, they would come over and call for her.

Tea time came and went, and the weather cooled. She had got to the stage of sewing in hooks and eyes and hemming the dress, when Simon tapped on the kitchen door, calling, 'Anyone home?' as he strode into the house.

'In here!' she called back from the sitting room. So he had not gone back to town without coming in to see her.

He stopped in the doorway, and with an unexpected rush of gladness she said, 'Hello.'

It was a moment before he spoke, so that she looked at him enquiringly. He seemed to be holding himself in, standing very still. 'Are you all right?' he said finally.

Surprised, she said, 'Yes, of course.'

He came slowly into the room. 'We expected you at home today.'

Sensing criticism, she said a little stiffly, 'I didn't think it was a firm arrangement. Anyway, you could have come over and fetched me if you wanted to.'

'I wasn't sure if you wanted to be— fetched.'

At a loss, she said, 'Well, I'm sorry. I've been busy.' She held up a part of the garment in her hands to show him how, and let it

drop back in her lap, the needle she had been
plying still in her fingers.

'What is it?' He put out a hand to lift some
of the pale apricot fabric.

'A dress. I might wear it on our honeymoon.'

He looked at her swiftly and let the material
fall from his hand and slither across her knee.
'That will be nice. May I see it on?'

'All right. Let me finish the hem, though.
Sit down.'

He took one of the other chairs and
watched her. 'Where are your parents?' he
asked.

'They went down to the club court for a
game of tennis. Would you like a drink or
anything?'

'No, thanks. You're very fast with that
needle.'

She glanced up, smiling. 'I'm quite domes-
ticated, you know. Well, that's why you
picked me for—to marry, isn't it?'

'Is it?' His brows rose. 'There were other
factors involved, actually.'

Yes, she thought, rescuing her from an
awkward situation for one, but once he had
done that he had realised that there would

be advantages in having her for a wife. She put in the last neat stitch, tied it off efficiently and broke the thread. Standing up, she said, 'I'll go and put it on. Won't be long.'

She tried it on in her own room, looking critically into the mirror. The narrow double straps over the shoulders, troublesome to make, looked good with her tan, and the sewn-in cummerbund effect nipped her waist, emphasising its slimness. The skirt length looked just right. She would press it after Simon had seen it.

Her hair was untidy, and she combed it quickly and put on a trace of pale apricot lipstick and slipped into a pair of white high-heeled sandals before returning to the living room.

She paused in the doorway, raised one arm and put the other on her hip, slinking across the carpet in exaggerated model style and doing a couple of swirling, hip-swinging turns before stopping a few feet from Simon's chair. 'Like it?' she asked him.

'Yes,' he said, 'I do.' He held out a hand. 'Come here.'

She didn't hesitate, letting him draw her down on to his lap. He ran his thumb over the ring he had given her, and she tucked her head under his chin, looking at their joined hands. His other hand stroked her upper arm, and then he moved his head and bent to kiss the smooth skin of her shoulder, his fingers tightening on her arm as he did so. He pushed her hair out of the way and kissed her nape, sending a delicate shiver all the way down her spine. Her half-closed eyes could see the tanned skin in the open neck of his shirt only inches away. One of her hands was trapped against his chest, but she freed the other from his light clasp and touched him with the tips of her fingers. The button constricted her tentative movement, and she heard him say in a low voice, 'Undo it.'

She obeyed blindly, flipping open the button, and the next, and the next, all the while feeling his hand soothing her shoulder and tracing the line of her spine. When she had undone his shirt to the waist, she hesitated in sudden shyness, and he said, 'Go on, darling. Touch me.'

His chest was hard and taut, and she explored it with fascination, pushing his collar aside to put her lips to his throat and slide them further down. His skin tasted slightly salty, and had a faint masculine fragrance.

When her hand reached his waist, he tugged gently at her hair to raise her face to him. Meredith closed her eyes and her lips parted, anticipating his kiss, but his mouth went first to the shallow groove below her ear, and then to her throat and the small hollow at its base.

She spread her fingers on his midriff, and felt him take a quick, uneven breath. She revelled in the movements of his mouth against her throat, her shoulder, then on the soft rise of her breast above the low front of her dress. His fingers slipped the flimsy strap down on to her arm, and his mouth opened against her skin, sending her pulses crazy. She felt him deftly part the single hook at her back, and begin to move the zip down, and she stiffened. 'What are you doing?' she demanded.

His head came up, and she saw the deepened colour under his tan, the glitter of desire behind the laughter in his eyes. 'Undressing you,' he said mildly. 'Do you mind?'

'Yes!' she said, indignant and flustered, and he laughed aloud and said, 'Why? You've just done it to me.'

She looked at his open shirt and took her hand away as though she'd been stung. 'That's different!' Her already flushed cheeks grew hotter.

'Why is it different, darling?' His voice was almost coaxing, but his eyes danced with humour.

'Because you're a man!' she snapped, trying to wriggle away from him. 'And I'm—not.'

He held her firmly, grinning with enjoyment. 'No, you're definitely not,' he agreed, 'and that's exactly why I'd like to look at you.'

'Look?' she asked with suspicious scorn.

'And perhaps a little more,' he admitted unblushingly. 'No?' He raised his brows enquiringly.

'No.' Her body ached to let him look and touch and do whatever he wanted, but her mind was horrified by her own wanton desire.

'We *are* engaged,' he reminded her.

'Yes, and this is my parents' house and they could be back any minute.'

'Do you think they'd be shocked?'

'I think *I'd* be very embarrassed.'

'I see.' Reluctantly he pulled the strap back up on her shoulder. 'I wouldn't want to see you embarrassed, Meredith.'

Well, she knew that. It was the reason they had got engaged in the first place. She made another effort to get off his knee, and this time he let her go.

'I'll go and take this dress off,' she muttered, really wanting an excuse to leave him and collect her thoughts.

'Now, that's just what I was suggesting a moment ago,' he said with mock reproach, 'and you wouldn't hear of it.'

Feeling safer now that she was no longer in his arms, she made a face at him and whisked out of the room to change.

Her parents returned shortly afterwards, and her mother made them supper—coffee and fresh scones which they ate while watching a drama on television. Afterwards Meredith went with Simon out to his car. A high moon sailed overhead, and the stars were thick and brilliant. There didn't seem to be any wind, and yet the pines that Meredith's father had planted on the rise beyond the milking shed ten years ago were whispering, and Meredith fancied that a faint whiff of their scent was discernible in the balmy night air.

Simon drew her into his arms and kissed her, and afterwards he kept her there close to him, his lips touching her hair. 'What were you and Michael talking about last night?' he murmured.

The question was so unexpected that it took a moment for her to even register it. 'Nothing,' she said, not wanting to think about it because the memory recalled the pain and frustrated anger she had experienced last night.

Simon held her a little away. The moonlight was so bright that she could see his face quite clearly, and it looked stern. 'Nothing?' he repeated dryly. 'You seemed upset. What happened?'

'Nothing happened!' she insisted crossly. She had been feeling remarkably contented, still mildly and pleasantly stimulated from their previous lovemaking, until he had brought this up. 'I asked him why he hadn't told me about his engagement sooner, and he—explained. That's all.'

'Satisfactory, was it?'

'Was what?' she asked obtusely.

'The explanation.'

'Oh, I suppose so. Only I couldn't——'

'Couldn't what?'

'Well,' she said rather tartly, 'I couldn't very well accuse him of letting me down when I was supposed to have become engaged to you without knowing about Francine, could I? So he was able to talk his way out of it quite nicely.'

'You mean you were spoiling for a fight and he wouldn't play?' Simon suggested.

On the verge of hotly denying it, she opened her mouth and said, 'I wasn't——'

But he was looking at her with such a quizzical expression that she stopped, sighed and admitted, 'Yes, I suppose so. Only Michael never did fight. He's got this exasperating habit of just clamming up and walking away when anyone gets angry with him. And then he won't talk to you until you've got over it.'

'Annoying,' Simon commented. He paused, and then said, 'Did he let you down very badly, Meredith?'

'What do you mean?'

'Well, you told me that you loved each other. Were you sure of that, or were you only guessing at his feelings?'

'We did love each other. He said he loved

me. I thought we'd be getting married when he finished his degree.'

'Had he asked you?'

'Well, not exactly, but it was taken for granted. At least, that's what I thought.'

'It doesn't do to take a man's feelings for granted,' Simon suggested gently. 'Especially if he only expresses them in the heat of passion.'

'No,' she said baldly. 'Well, I know now, don't I?'

She shivered, although it wasn't cold, and he put his hand on her arm and said, 'You'd better go in. How about staying in town after work tomorrow, and we'll go out for dinner?'

'That would be nice.'

'Good. I'll call you.'

He brushed her cheek with his lips and gave her a little push towards the house before climbing into the car.

She didn't sleep well, but lay in her bed under a single sheet feeling sticky and hot. Her skin still remembered the touch of Simon's hands and lips, and thinking of them made her go even hotter. When she was with him she forgot to grieve for Michael, and his kisses left no room for thoughts of any other man. But seeing Michael again last night had brought back the pain of her loss. She recalled the feel of his hand tugging her down the steps, the way they had moved together on the dance floor as though their bodies were one. It had been Michael for so long she still couldn't believe, when he held her in his arms, that it was over, both of them irrevocably committed to someone else.

Irrevocably? Engagements can be broken, she had said to Simon on that first day. And he had agreed.

Supposing Michael broke his engagement—or Francine did? They said it had been a whirlwind romance, they didn't really know each other very well. Maybe it was only an infatuation after all. Michael might change his mind. And if he did——

If he did, where did that leave her while she was engaged to Simon—possibly even married to him? She didn't know when Michael and Francine planned to get married, she hadn't heard a date mentioned. Suddenly January seemed far too early a date for her own wedding to Simon.

Fear clutched at her stomach as she turned

restlessly in the bed. She couldn't break her promise to Simon, could she? But could she bear to marry him if Michael were free? Thinking of Michael, she felt tears trickling down her cheeks on to the pillow. She thought back to the very first time he had kissed her, when they had been still at school, their mutual astonishment, changing quickly to delight, at the realisation that their childhood fondness for each other was turning into something else, something infinitely more exciting and grown-up. All the wonderful times they had enjoyed, before he went away, and in the holidays whenever he had managed to come home rather than work in Auckland to augment his university grants. Usually they were with a crowd of other young people, his sister Debra, Anneke, and others of their age group, but she and Michael had always been a pair within the group. It was understood. Sometimes they had been teased, but they would only smile at each other and shrug it off. Their friends weren't unkind, and she and Michael had been so sure of each other that it hadn't mattered. When he was away some of the other boys would invite her out occasionally, but they knew she was

Michael's girl, and accepted that for them she had only friendship and perhaps a cool good night kiss on her doorstep when they delivered her home.

She had written to him regularly—lighthearted, newsy letters and not sentimental, because it wasn't in her nature to commit her deepest feelings to paper, but always signed, 'With love'. Michael was not a good correspondent, and she knew he had to spend a lot of time studying, but she had treasured his short, scrawled, intermittent replies, and the odd humorous card he sent. They had always laughed at the same things, and Michael loved a joke.

She had thought they were made for each other. Everything had seemed so right. Until Francine came along. And now there was the complication of Simon, too. Had she been foolish, consenting to make their engagement a real one? And could she back out of it now? Simon's lovemaking was exciting, but there was more to marriage than that. Sex wasn't love, and if she really loved Michael, would sex be enough to tie her to Simon?

And of course she loved Michael. Simon must know that. She remembered the way he had studied her face last night when he came looking for her. He knew, and he was carefully ignoring it, giving her time to get over it. And sometimes she thought she had— when Simon kissed her and stroked her the way he had this afternoon. And yet the thought of Michael could bring tears. Maybe she was doing the wrong thing, maybe she had gone thankfully into Simon's arms simply because his experienced kisses stimulated a physical response which put her mind on hold and stopped her thinking about Michael. And surely that was a shaky basis for marriage?

Her head began to throb. Her mind was running in circles, getting nowhere. She thought about getting up for an aspirin. Perhaps Simon would help, she was seeing him tomorrow. But Simon was part of the problem, she couldn't ask him to solve it for her. She was getting confused, and sleepy at last. She thought of Simon again as her breathing slowed and deepened. But later in the night she dreamed of Michael. It was an unhappy dream, the details of which she didn't remember when she woke, only that she had been weeping, accusing him of breaking something of hers—perhaps they had been children again, it wasn't clear—but he hadn't cared, he had walked away from her, saying, 'Simon will fix it. Leave me alone.'

Well, it didn't take Freud to work that one out, she thought as she dressed for the office in the morning. Only she wasn't sure if Simon could fix her broken heart. She didn't know if anyone could.

CHAPTER SIX

AT lunch time on Monday Meredith was down town, looking for Christmas presents, when she met Debra Kingsley crossing the stone-paved mall in the main shopping centre.

'I hardly had a chance to talk to you at the party,' Debra said. 'Did you enjoy it?'

'Yes, lovely,' Meredith answered automatically.

'Have you had lunch? Let's have something together, shall we?'

'Actually I meant to skip lunch. I have to get back to work in fifteen minutes.'

'That won't do you any good,' Debra said firmly. 'Come on, we'll nip into the coffee bar here and you can have a sandwich, anyway.'

When they were settled at a corner table with sandwiches and drinks, Debra said, 'Now, tell me about Simon.'

'What about him?' Meredith asked warily.

'Well, how you got engaged to him, of course! I don't see you with the old crowd now, and I could hardly pump you at Michael's party in front of Simon. You

113

certainly kept it quiet—nobody had any idea about him.'

'I did,' Meredith said briefly, feeling her way.

'Of course, you've been living next door to him, or near enough, haven't you? Anneke said she should have realised ages ago, only we all thought it was you and Michael. Oh, I know Michael always pooh-poohed the idea of anything really serious——'

Meredith's head lifted.

'—but Mum was the only one who believed him. She always said he shouldn't even be thinking seriously about any girl until he'd finished his degree. And you know Michael, he's the biddable one of the family. Took her advice to heart, finished his studies, and then—wham! Got engaged to a girl we'd never seen before. I think it's the only time Mum's been surprised by anything he did. She took it well, though, and she really likes Francine. They've been getting on like wildfire.'

'She seems a nice girl.'

'Yes, we all like her. I was a bit disappointed at first because I'd always supposed it would be you, and I'd thought the only reason Michael downplayed your friendship was because Mum wouldn't have approved if she'd realised how close you and he were. I used to try and keep quiet about how much you saw of each other, thinking I was aiding the cause. But I guess the two of you really were telling the truth about being "just good friends", weren't you?'

Meredith smiled, not caring to answer that. So Michael had given his family the impression that she wasn't serious. An upsurge of the anger she felt with him when she wasn't feeling sorry for herself made her hand shake as she picked up a sandwich. But fairness compelled her to think again. Perhaps that really was how he had viewed their relationship. It certainly hadn't been as important to him as she had always assumed.

'Well, and what about Simon, then?' Debra persisted. 'Come on, you can tell me all.'

'There's not much to tell, honestly. I've known Simon all my life. We've always been fond of each other, but I suppose I was too young for him before.'

'You mean he was waiting for you to grow up? Daddy-Long-Legs and all that?'

'Don't be an idiot! He's not *that* much

older. Anyway, he was married for years, and I wasn't even eighteen when his wife died.'

'Oh, yes, I remember. Awful, wasn't it? One doesn't imagine people dying in child-birth these days. And she was so gorgeous. I met her a couple of times. Don't you mind that he's been married before?'

'No, I don't mind.'

'Mm, I suppose the practice might even make him a better husband. You'll be looking after his little boy, too, I suppose.'

'Yes. I'm looking forward to it.'

She was making all the right responses, but what she really wanted was to pump Debra about her brother and his fiancée. How was the engagement going? Did Debra think they were really in love? Was Michael happy? Here was her opportunity to settle some of the doubts of last night, but instead of taking it she was finding herself less and less able to ask the necessary questions. When she carefully steered the conversation back to Michael and Francine and their plans, she learned that they were both in Auckland, staying with Francine's people. All Debra could tell her about a wedding date was that they were going to discuss it with Francine's parents.

The fifteen minutes sped by and Meredith had found out nothing. For all Debra's chatter, she wasn't really a very informative person.

Meredith was quiet throughout the dinner with Simon. After they had finished eating he asked for the bill and said, 'Coffee at my place, okay?'

Meredith nodded and picked up her bag. The restaurant was pleasant, but inevitably their conversation wasn't really private. She had felt inhibited all evening. She was restless, unsettled and unsure of herself, and when they got out in the fresh air she took a deep breath and said, 'I'd really like a walk.'

'We could go down to the waterfront and then come back to the car.'

'Yes,' she said. 'Please.'

They walked in silence, and Meredith set quite a brisk pace, wanting to clear her head. Standing on the bridge overlooking the long inlet where sea-going yachts, some from faraway countries, lay idly at anchor, she watched the slight movement of the masts against the starry sky and sighed.

'What is it?' Simon asked. His hand covered hers on the concrete parapet.

'Oh, nothing,' she said. 'Wouldn't it be nice to just get on a boat and sail away?'

'As I remember,' he said drily, 'you're not likely to enjoy that very much.'

He had done quite a bit of sailing, and once when Anneke and she were about fifteen they had been on a day trip with him and Jill and a male friend on the friend's yacht. For Meredith it had been a once-in-a-lifetime experience. As soon as they left the harbour mouth and entered slightly choppier waters she had begun to feel queasy, and she never did acquire her 'sea-legs', as Simon's friend had optimistically promised she would in an hour or two. Eventually Simon took pity on her and insisted that they cut the trip short, and even though she had bravely protested at spoiling the day for the others, she was infinitely relieved to sight dry land again.

'It's not fair to remind me,' she complained now.

'Someone has to curb your romantic flights of fancy. Supposing I took you at your word and booked a cruise for our honeymoon?'

Meredith looked away, down at the

shimmering water below them. She felt his puzzled gaze on her bent head. 'Ready to go back now?' he asked.

'Yes.' She turned without looking at him and walked by his side, her hand tucked into his arm. They were walking as lovers, but she felt far apart from him, engrossed in her own dark and not entirely coherent thoughts.

At his house he made her sit in the living room while he brewed coffee. He served it with a dish of chocolate mints wrapped in green foil, and she unwrapped one, put it in her mouth, and sat smoothing the little tinsel square on her knee until he said, 'Your fingers are going green.'

She looked at them, and they were. She screwed up the foil and put it back in the dish.

'Drink your coffee,' Simon advised, and she picked up the pottery mug and obeyed him. He waited until she had finished, then put his own mug down on the floor beside his chair and said, 'Something's wrong, isn't it? Are you going to tell me?'

She looked at him almost fearfully, her empty cup clasped in her lap between both hands. 'I'm not sure if I'm—if we're—doing the right thing,' she said. 'Getting married.'

For a long moment he sat looking at her in silence. Then he said deliberately, 'I'm sure it's right for me. What you mean is, you don't know if it's right for you.'

'Yes,' she said almost inaudibly.

After another pause he said, 'This wouldn't have surprised me yesterday, after Michael's party. But then you were talking quite happily about making that dress for our honeymoon. I thought you'd realised you don't really care for him.'

'Of *course* I care for him!' she said fiercely, looking up. 'Do you think I could just forget him in a few weeks when I've been in love with him for *years*?'

His eyes were coolly assessing. 'No, I suppose not. Perhaps I've been expecting too much. But we both knew the situation when you agreed to marry me. So what's changed?'

'Nothing, I suppose. Only I——' She stopped uncomfortably. 'I think I was still sort of in shock when I said I'd marry you.'

'No, you weren't. You'd got over the shock, you'd had time to think and were perfectly calm and rational.'

'How would you know?' she demanded,

and he smiled.

'I know you, Meredith. What you mean is, you've had second thoughts since. Was it something Michael said on Saturday night? He'd had a fair bit to drink, you know. I wouldn't take too much notice of any sentimental sweet nothings he might have whispered in your ear for old times' sake.'

'He didn't! I told you, we almost had a quarrel.'

'Yes,' he said thoughtfully, 'and a very juvenile one it sounded like, too.'

'You don't know that! You don't even know what happened.'

'Nothing, according to your supposedly reliable evidence. Did he kiss you?'

'No! And if he'd tried I wouldn't have let him. He's engaged to someone else.'

'And so are you. Or had that slipped your mind?'

'No, it had *not* slipped my mind!' she snapped. 'But I'm beginning to think it was a mistake! Which is the point I was trying to make.'

Simon was staring at her with some concentration. He looked grim and cold, almost as though he disliked her. She had never had a serious disagreement with Simon before. It was a horrible feeling. 'Oh, Simon,' she said, her voice wobbling, 'I don't want to fight with you. I didn't mean it to be like this.'

His face softened and he held out his hand to her. 'Come here,' he said.

She shook her head. In his arms she would forget her doubts and misgivings, but that was only temporary. When he left her she would be prey to them again, and nothing would be resolved.

Simon left his chair and came over to hers, removing the coffee mug from her grasp to deposit it on a side table, pulling her up with his hands on her arms, ignoring her resistance.

'No, don't!' she said, even as he drew her close and lifted her chin with one firm hand.

'Come on,' he coaxed. 'Kiss and make up, Meredith.'

'But I have to to talk to——'

'Afterwards.' His mouth closed over hers, and in moments she yielded to its seductive persuasion and opened her lips to him.

They stayed locked together for a long time, and when he stopped kissing her he didn't release her but let her bury her head against his shoulder while he held her, his hand running gently up and down her back.

'There's no mistake about *that*, is there, my darling?' he enquired with tender triumph, a thread of amusement in his voice.

'There's more to marriage than making love,' she managed to say, her voice muffled against his shirt.

'True,' he conceded.

'People should be sure,' she pursued doggedly. 'And January—it's not a very long engagement, is it?'

'No. But we've known each other for a long time. You seemed quite happy about it, I thought.'

'I know, but—well, it's closer now. Nearly Christmas. Couldn't we wait just a little while?'

He moved, holding her away from him so that he could see her face. 'How long?'

'I don't know,' she answered vaguely. 'Until—well, until I'm sure.'

'You were sure before. Now you're not so sure. You could be sure and unsure again. This could go on for years.'

'Of course not! I'll know when—I mean,

in a few months—in April, perhaps, or
May——'

'Or June or July, or pie-in-the-sky,' he said
scornfully. '*When*, Meredith? Give me a date!'

'I can't!' She jerked herself out of his
hold, glaring at him. 'I don't know the date
of——'

'Of what?' He stared as she hesitated and
looked away from him, flushing wildly. 'It's
something to do with *Michael*, isn't it?' He
frowned, his keen brain working it out. 'You
don't know the date of—his *wedding*?'

He looked disbelieving and accusing at the
same time, and her silence convicted her. He
moved away suddenly, jamming his hands
into his pockets as though to stop himself
from doing something violent to her. When
he turned to face her from several feet away,
the anger in his eyes frightened her. He said
roughly, 'For God's sake, Meredith, *grow up*!
You can't have your cake and eat it too. If
you really don't want to go through with
marrying me while there's a slim chance that
Michael might be free again, then we'll break
it off here and now. One thing I'm not going
to do is hang about waiting for you to decide
on me as a second option once Michael's out

of your reach for good. What exactly do you think I am?'

'I'm—I'm sorry,' she said miserably. The way he put it, what she had been trying to do sounded monstrous. No person would have put up with it, and she couldn't blame him for being furious. She hadn't thought it through in precisely those terms, but basically he had hit the nail on the head, and she was ashamed to own what had been in her mind. 'I didn't think of it like that,' she said in a low voice.

He brushed the feeble excuse aside. 'Well?' he asked harshly. 'Do we call it off, or go on with the wedding—as planned?'

He had never spoken to her in that tone before. Raising startled and wary eyes to his face she said, 'Wouldn't you care?'

He looked, if anything, even more angry at that. 'You know exactly how much I'd care,' he said flatly. 'No more games, please, Meredith. You'd better make a real decision, this time. And think carefully, because I warn you, this is your last chance. If we're going to be married, I'm not letting you change your mind again. And if you decide to back out now, don't expect me to be around waiting for you after Michael marries Francine. It's either one or the other, a genuine commitment, or a clean break and a final one.'

'An ultimatum?'

'Yes.' His voice was curt, unyielding. 'I'm sorry, but I can't go on living with this kind of uncertainty. I'd rather know—now.'

She would lose his friendship, everything. They had gone too far now to return to the old easy, platonic footing. A clean and final break, he had said, but they would still see each other from time to time, it was inevitable with their two families as close as they were. And there would always be this between them, a barrier impossible to cross. How that would hurt. Unbearably. Even worse than losing Michael.

Was that possible? She would lose them both, then, because the chances of Michael's engagement being broken seemed pretty slim. Simon was here, and Michael wasn't. Was that why Simon seemed at the moment so much more important, why his loss would matter more than anything in the world? Her mind skittered here and there trying to find a way out, but there wasn't one. Simon was waiting for her to answer him, the silence thunderous with tension.

Her voice raw and uneven, she said, 'I'll marry you in January, Simon—as planned.'

She thought he would take her in his arms again, but he didn't. His shoulders might have relaxed a little, but his face hadn't changed. 'Right,' he said. 'You're quite certain this time?'

'Quite certain.' She managed to steady her voice and it came out low and clear.

He regarded her for a moment longer, almost broodingly, then said abruptly, 'It's time I took you home.'

He didn't even kiss her good night when they got there, and she went in feeling rather like a disgraced child. He had practically called her one, tonight, fed up with her immature behaviour. Well, he had cause, she supposed. She really ought to have known better. And this time there was no going back. Simon didn't mean to let her break her promise. She knew, somehow, that he was perfectly capable of enforcing it.

Christmas was a family affair. Simon and Meredith, with Benjy, divided their time between the two farmhouses, and sometimes both families were at one place or the other. Meredith's brother Ian, and his wife and two-year-old daughter came down from Paihia in the far north where he was an engineer with the Electricity Department, and stayed over Christmas and Boxing Day. Christmas dinner featured the traditional turkey and ham, but they ate it cold with salads, although the fruit puddings that Mrs Townsend had made were heated and served with cream and ice cream on top.

On the evening of Boxing Day they all went over to the Van Dyk's for a barbecue. The fire was lit in a brick, home-built grate made by Mr Van Dyk years ago, and soon the succulent aroma of sizzling steaks and chops mingled with the scent of jasmine and honeysuckle growing on the trellis that sheltered the barbecue area. The two married members of the Van Dyk family had brought their respective families, and the children were mostly running about on the lawn playing chase, but Benjy was helping Meredith's small niece to straddle a tricycle and volunteering to push her. Simon and Meredith, sitting on a wooden seat in front of the trellis, watched with some amusement.

'He's awfully good with her,' Meredith commented.

'Yes, he seems to have taken quite a fancy to her.'

'Perhaps he'd like a little sister.'

He looked at her. 'Perhaps,' he said, 'but I hope you're not going to be in too much of a hurry to provide him with one.'

Surprised, she glanced up at him. 'Why?' she asked blankly. She had thought he would welcome brothers and sisters for Benjy. He wanted the boy to have a normal home and family, surely?

'I told you,' he said, 'I'd like you to myself for a while.'

'Steaks are ready!' someone called from the barbecue. 'Come and get it!' And Simon took her hand and pulled her up, saying, 'Come on, I'm hungry.'

She had the feeling he hadn't wanted a discussion on the subject, but the following week, on New Year's Day, he brought it up himself.

They had been for a walk, along a rough country road winding between tall totara and gum trees at the edge of scrubby farmland,

and as they retraced their steps back to her home, his arm about her shoulders and hers at his waist, he said suddenly, 'Meredith— are you on the pill?'

She stopped abruptly, her arm dropping as she turned to face him with startled eyes. 'No!' she said. 'Of course not!'

He smiled a little ruefully. 'I'm sorry, darling, but there isn't any "of course" about it, you know. It's fairly normal these days, and—there was Michael. I thought you might have——'

'Well, I didn't!' she said, adding fiercely, 'Though I sometimes wish that I had. It might have made a difference.'

'I doubt it,' he said. 'Anyway, I'm selfish enough to be glad that I'll be the first for you—won't I?'

'Yes,' she muttered, looking away. There had never been anyone else, really, except Michael, and now Simon. 'I thought you'd have known.'

'I thought I did, but I couldn't be sure, without asking.' He hesitated. 'Only, if you're not on the pill,' he said carefully, 'one of us will have to do something. Do you want me to take care of it? I don't mind, but the choice is limited for men, and not so reliable.'

'No,' she said, 'it's all right. I'll see my doctor, or there's a clinic in town.' He was determined, it seemed, not to start a family right away. She said uncertainly, 'We *will* have children, won't we, Simon?'

'I have a son,' he reminded her.

Raising shocked eyes to his face, she said, 'But—surely you'd like a real family? Didn't you and Jill plan to have more than one child?'

'You're not Jill!' he said, hurting her more than he could possibly know. 'You don't have to try and take her place.'

'I *wouldn't* try,' she said shakily. 'But *I* want children. Don't you think Benjy should have brothers and sisters? He's accustomed to living in a large family.'

'There's plenty of time for that,' Simon said easily. 'He's going to have enough adjusting to do in the first year or so without having to cope with a baby in the family as well. And that goes for you, too.'

'Well, in a year or so, then?' she persisted. 'Benjy will be at school. I'll have more time and he'll have new interests—it could be the ideal time.'

But Simon wouldn't commit himself. 'Maybe,' he said. 'We can talk about it then.'

CHAPTER SEVEN

'HAVE you asked for time off for our honey-moon?' Simon asked Meredith as they unwrapped an early wedding present at her home a few days later.

'I've given in my notice,' she answered, staring a little. 'You didn't expect me to keep on working, did you?'

He folded the flowered pink paper carefully. 'I thought you might want to carry on for a while. Don't you like your job?'

'Yes, but Benjy will need me.'

'Not immediately. Won't you be bored with nothing to do?'

'There's plenty to do. I want to get the house organised first.'

He grinned. 'Is my house so bad? I thought I was quite a good housekeeper.'

'I don't mean that it's dirty or anything,' she said hastily. 'Only I'd like to make it more—homely. If you don't mind, that is.'

'Of course I don't mind. I expect it needs a woman's touch. And naturally you'll want to put your own personal stamp on the place.

You've got a fairly strong nesting instinct, haven't you?'

Perhaps she had. Certainly she had no great career ambitions. Her work was interesting and satisfying, and she had liked being in charge of the office, but she had always assumed that marriage and a family would be a welcome interruption to her business life, even if she picked up the threads again when the children were grown.

She held up the copper-bottomed pan with the turned wooden handle that his sister Katie and her husband had sent them, and said, 'This will brighten up your kitchen.'

'Our kitchen,' he corrected her, smiling.

'Our kitchen,' she echoed obediently. 'Have you got the card there? I'll write a thank-you note tonight.'

For her wedding dress she had chosen classic white lace in a simple style that let the fabric take the limelight, with a fitted, scoop-necked bodice, short scalloped sleeves and a hemline that showed her ankles in the front, dipping to a short train at the back. Her veil was a circle of matching lace, and when she fixed it over the Grecian knot into which she had twisted her long hair on her wedding morning, she thought she looked remarkably elegant, quite different from her everyday self.

The other remarkable thing, she decided, was her lack of nerves. In spite of her earlier misgivings, as the wedding date had drawn nearer she grew more calm and more certain that in marrying Simon she was doing the right thing. She was less excited than her parents. Her mother kept darting into her room, exclaiming, 'Oh, darling, did we remember to . . . ?' Meredith and Anneke, who was helping her dress before getting into her own bridesmaid's dress of pastel blue chiffon, soothed her down time and again with assurances that nothing had been forgotten. And her father had been pacing the floor for ages before she emerged from her room walking slowly and holding her train off the floor.

'Well,' he said, staring as she came towards him, and clearing his throat. 'Well, here you are at last.'

Meredith laughed at him. 'I'm dead on time, Dad. We've got easily half an hour to get to the church.'

'Well,' he said for the third time. 'You're

looking very lovely, Merrie. I'm proud of you.'

She kissed his cheek. 'I hope Simon will be, too.'

'Couldn't have a more beautiful bride.'

He had once, though. She pushed the barbed thought away. 'You're prejudiced,' she said lightly. 'Where's Mum?'

Her mother came in then, adjusting the silk pillbox hat that matched the primrose pink dress and coat she was wearing. 'Oh, you do look lovely, dear,' she said, echoing her husband. 'Simon's a lucky man.'

'Don't forget to tell him so,' Meredith suggested, laughing.

A car horn sounded outside, and her mother said, 'Oh, there's Maria and Frans.' She was driving to the church with Simon's parents. 'Good luck, darling.' She pecked Meredith's cheek and rushed to the door. 'Don't keep him waiting too long.'

Meredith had no intention of keeping Simon waiting at all. He would be there on time, she was sure. The Van Dyks' car had barely reached the end of the drive when she said to her father and Anneke, 'All right. Let's go.'

Simon's family were members of the local Presbyterian church, it being close to the Dutch Reformed faith they had followed in the Netherlands. But he had not minded their getting married in the Anglican church Meredith had attended since childhood. He was standing with his back to her as she walked down the aisle on her father's arm, but when they were nearly there he turned and smiled at her, and she smiled back with great confidence. He looked very handsome in grey with a dark blue tie, and when the ceremony got to the point where he took her hand and placed the ring on her finger, he smiled at her again, and she felt her heart make a tiny revolution of pure happiness. When Anneke stepped forward to fold back her veil, he put out his hand to help, and then looked down at her face with an intent stare as though she was an Eastern bride who had been presented to her husband sight unseen. She gave him a tentative, slightly puzzled smile, hoping he liked what he saw, and he bent quickly and kissed her very lightly. A ripple of approval passed around the church, and the minister smiled broadly as he brought the ceremony to a close.

Afterwards they had a reception in the district hall, decorated the night before by their respective families with flowers and fronds of silver-backed ponga ferns. The speeches were kept to a minimum, the food was magnificent, provided by a local playcentre committee who catered for various functions in order to raise funds for their expenses, and as the afternoon wore on the proceedings moved away from formality in the general direction of hilarity. A long and not entirely truthful song in Dutch and English, purporting to tell all about Simon's courtship of Meredith, was received with much laughter and many helpful interjections. When it was finished, a group began singing traditional Dutch songs, the leader of the impromptu glee club exhorting the other guests to join in. Even the Kiwis made valiant efforts to follow the words, and afterwards started up some singing of their own, helped by guitar music played by one of the Maori guests.

It was all great fun, and back at the house the celebrations continued unabated. Meredith had become accustomed, through her friendship with the Van Dyk family, to the enormous and surprising capacity of the supposedly sober and stolid Dutch for enjoying themselves. They loved a celebration, whether for a birthday, a wedding, or an anniversary, and Dutch parties were occasions of great rejoicing, long and loud and innocently uninhibited. In that sense they reminded her of the Maori people, whose parties sometimes went on for days, until everyone was simply exhausted from having a good time.

In the Netherlands the wedding celebrations would have lasted nearly a week, but here things were different, and although the guests would remain for a while after the departure of the bride and groom, tomorrow they would all have gone.

'Shall we see if we can slip off?' Simon asked her at about five o'clock.

'We'd be lucky!' she grinned at him, knowing that there was small chance of their making it without being noticed. 'But I'll go and get changed, anyway.'

'I'll alert Ian,' he said. Ian had been detailed to hide Simon's car and produce it at the appropriate moment for a quick getaway. 'Your brother is a serious, sensible married man,' Simon had told her when they discussed the subject. 'I'd trust him not to fill the cases with confetti, paint JUST MARRIED on the boot, or tie old shoes to the bumper. Which is more than I can say for any of my mad Dutch relations.'

Ian wasn't particularly serious, but he could be trusted to keep a promise, and did what was required of him. Twenty minutes afterwards, when Meredith had changed into a straw-coloured linen skirt and a sleeveless tan silk top with a matching shirt-jacket, he drew the car up at the door and they made a run for it.

Ian held the passenger door open for Meredith, and Simon slipped smartly into the driver's seat, just dodging a shower of confetti. Grinning, he put his foot on the accelerator and sped down the drive, rounding the corner on to the road so fast that she was thrown against him. 'Sorry,' he said, glancing in the rear vision mirror. 'Put your safety belt on.'

'I'll need it, with a driver like you!' she laughed, snapping the buckle closed.

'Watch it, *wife*. I don't need to stand for that sort of cheek from you.' His glance was teasing, and she grimaced back, hiding her sudden delight at the word 'wife'.

'Ee-uch!' she said expressively. 'I've married a male chauvinist pig! Now you're showing your true colours.'

'That's right.' He continued in a sinister tone, 'I have you in my power. You cannot escape me now, my little bird!'

Meredith giggled. 'Oh, woe is me!' she wailed, wringing her hands theatrically. 'Whatever will become of me?'

'Do you really want to know?' He hadn't stopped smiling, but his eyes changed as they roamed explicitly over her body, and she choked, blushing furiously. 'Don't do that!'

He laughed, then looked again in the rear vision mirror and slowed down a little. 'Nobody seems to have followed us.' He fumbled for his seat belt, brought the diagonal strap half way over his body and said, 'Can you fasten it, please?'

She reached over him, grasping the buckle. The belt stuck, and she felt the warmth of his chest against her knuckles before she lifted the wide strip of webbing away to pull it smoothly from its housing and clicked the buckle into place.

'Thanks,' he said, raising his left hand and caressing her nape. 'That's a very fancy hairdo. Rather inhibiting.'

'Don't you like it?' she asked anxiously.

'Yes, I do. It's very nice, and you made a ravishing bride, very, very beautiful. Only I'm afraid to touch your hair in case I spoil it.'

'Well, I have to take it out sometime,' she said, putting up her hand to pull out the pins.

'No.' His warm fingers closed over hers, taking them to his lips. 'Not now,' he said, his voice lowering. 'Later.'

She quivered at the touch of his mouth, and then he turned her palm and buried his lips warmly, briefly, in its hollow. He shot her a look before returning his attention to the road and letting go of her hand. She clasped it with the other one in her lap. What she had seen in his eyes was exciting and almost frightening. The nerves that had not bothered her before began to make themselves felt. Simon was a passionate man, she had realised that in the last few weeks although he had restrained his demands for her sake, as she well knew. Now there was no reason for holding back. They were married and he would expect her to reciprocate his passion.

With a few words, a touch, he had dispelled the lighthearted atmosphere with which they had started the journey, and now the small space in the car was filled with sexual tension.

She took a quick, unsteady breath. 'Where are we going?'

He glanced at her and said, 'Would you believe—I've hired a yacht to sail around the Bay of Islands?'

She cast him an indignant look. 'No, I wouldn't! Don't tease.'

Simon grinned and relented. 'Okay. We're going to a bach in the back of beyond—way up north. It used to be a farm cottage, but some friends of a friend bought it for a holiday place a couple of years back. They've kindly agreed to rent it to us for a couple of weeks. There's a tiny beach, a lot of bush, and damn all else. Suit you?'

He knew it would, she loved the bush and the sea, and the solitude sounded delightful.

'Lovely,' she said. 'What do we do for food?'

'There's a store five miles from the bach. The storekeeper is leaving a box of groceries and some milk at his back door for us tonight, and we can go back in shopping hours when we need more.'

He had thought of everything. The tension began to ease, and she started chatting about the wedding. 'It went off very well, didn't it?' she said. 'I don't envy Mum and Dad the cleaning up, though.'

'They'll have help. Who was that extraordinary lady in the purple hat with the peacock feathers?'

'Mum's Auntie Grace. My great-aunt. Wonderful, isn't she?'

'I'd no idea you had such exotic relations. We had a fascinating conversation about psychic emanations and their effect on the revolutions of the planets—not just Earth, all the planets.'

'Is that what she's on about now? Last time I saw her—at Ian's wedding—she was telling everyone about hydroponic plant-growing. She's quite sane, actually, she just gets terribly enthusiastic about things and tends to have a one-track mind. Once she had this absolute fixation about starting a secret society to rid the world of nuclear scientists. She was quite serious.'

'She was very serious about the psychic emanations, too. I wish I'd had longer to listen to her.'

'I don't know how you managed to get away. She's a bit of a terror for buttonholing people. We always have to keep an eye on her and watch out for glassy-eyed reluctant listeners who need to be tactfully removed. I saw Mum rescue Michael from her today. He looked positively dazed. I don't think he's met anyone quite like Auntie Grace before.'

He looked at her quickly. 'Did you talk to Michael at all?'

'For a while.' She turned to him. 'It's all right,' she said.

She had seen Michael in the church as she walked out on Simon's arm, and her heart had given a familiar little lurch, almost a reflex action. Francine was not with him, although the invitation had included her. Afterwards she had seen him in the crowd outside the church as the wedding party posed for photographs, and for a few minutes she had watched him as he talked to someone, throwing back his dark handsome head to laugh at something they said. And she had felt Simon's arm under her hand, looked up into Simon's questioning eyes—and forgotten Michael. Later she had talked to him, let him

wish her well and tease her a little, and
realised that the hurt had gone. She could
look him in the eye, smile at him without
constraint, speak of Francine without the
hidden bitterness of jealousy burning inside,
even receive without a blink the news that
their wedding would take place in March.
She had wished him good luck and meant it.
'I hope you'll be very happy.' It had been all
right.

Simon took her hand in his, his eyes
searching for a moment. 'Good,' he said.

They stopped in the prosperous and pretty
northern town of Kaitaia, the last outpost of
trade and industry before the long road that
led up the narrow neck of land to the tip of
the island, Cape Reinga, where, according to
Maori legend, the souls of the departed leaped
into the sea.

'Hungry?' Simon asked her.

'A bit. I don't feel like a proper meal,
though.' The food at the reception had been
rich and filling.

'We'll have something light,' he promised.

They settled for a salad-filled bread roll
each and real fruit juice made from Kerikeri

oranges. Afterwards they strolled around the darkening town to stretch their legs before climbing back into the car.

'Not far now,' Simon assured her, and handed her a map. 'Watch out for that road, it goes off on the right a few miles further on.'

By the time they left the main highway, the night was closing in, and they travelled several more kilometres before coming upon a small country store-cum-post office beside a neatly fenced bungalow.

Simon got out and went round to the back of the store, returning with a box of groceries.

'How do we pay for it?' she asked.

'Slipped a cheque under the door. He left the docket in the box.'

The countryside was quiet, the drowsing hills barely visible now except for the odd shaggy macracarpa or misshapen pine rearing on the horizon. White blobs of sheep lay in the paddocks on either side of the road, and sometimes their eyes glowed eerily in the headlights.

When at last Simon drew up outside a small, square cottage, Meredith was almost asleep.

She helped him carry their bags and the groceries, and he pulled out a key and fumbled the door open, feeling round the corner for the light. Meredith blinked as it came on, and he pushed her gently before him.

'Sorry,' he said. 'I should have carried you, I suppose.'

'That's for when we get home, isn't it?' She looked about them and noted with pleasure the simple comfort of seagrass matting on the floor, a cane lounge suite with Indian cotton cushions, a divan covered with cheery printed fabric, a table and chairs in one corner and a tiled servery bench dividing the main room from the kitchen.

Exploring further, she found a separate bedroom with a comfortable-looking double bed, a small, sparkling bathroom with shower and toilet, and a tiny laundry holding a single sink and a washing machine. She opened a couple of windows just a slit, so that they wouldn't be invaded by insects.

'It's got everything,' she said to Simon as he placed their cases on the bed.

'No TV,' he said. 'Do you mind?'

She shook her head. 'Who wants to watch

TV?'

'My sentiments exactly.' He reached a hand out to her but she evaded him, pretending not to see, and said, 'Is there a jar of coffee in those groceries? I want a cup. What about you?'

'Mmm. I'd like a quick shower first, I think. I won't take long.'

'Is there hot water?'

'The people at the farm will have turned it on for us, I hope.' He opened the catch of his case and flipped up the lid.

Meredith was in the kitchen boiling the kettle when Simon, wearing dark blue pyjama pants with no top, came back into the living area. She had unpacked the supplies, putting the tins and packets into cupboards, pouring milk into a jug she had found. There were plates, cups, cutlery and cooking utensils in cupboards and drawers, and some tins for tea and sugar.

She poured hot water into the cups, sugared her own and added a little milk to his, then carried them both over to the little table next to the windows.

'Is there a sea view in the daytime?' she asked him.

'Just. You can glimpse it through the trees. It's two minutes' walk to the beach.' He leaned over to open one of the windows a little. 'Listen.'

The hushed murmur of the waves invaded the cottage, and Meredith smiled. 'Lovely. I'll sleep well tonight.'

He glanced at her, his eyes carrying an unmistakable message, and she dipped her head hastily and concentrated on stirring her coffee.

They hardly spoke as they drank, and as soon as she had finished he took the cup from her and carried it with his to the sink. 'I'll wash them,' he said.

'I'll unpack and have a shower, then.'

There was a built-in wardrobe, and a dressing table with drawers, and she saw that Simon had already used one of the drawers and stowed his case in the bottom of the wardrobe. Her head had begun to throb slightly, and as she started emptying her case, she wished she had thought to bring some aspirin. It wasn't very late but she had never been a good traveller, and she felt slightly queasy as well as suddenly exhausted. She thought of asking Simon if he had any pain relievers, but was fairly sure he wouldn't have, and besides, she cringed at the prospect of starting her honeymoon by announcing to her bridegroom that she had a headache. Simon would probably laugh, and she didn't want that tonight. She had intended to be a sophisticated and receptive bride. Perhaps she would feel better after her shower.

Her hair remained pinned, so she didn't need a shower cap. A few tendrils escaped and lay wetly on her shoulders when she emerged, but she rubbed them dry briskly and they had gone feathery by the time she had used a scented body lotion on her skin. Her head was aching in earnest now, and she hopefully opened the cupboard over the washbasin, but it held only a packet of wound dressings and an unopened cake of soap. She sighed and donned the special nightdress she had bought for tonight. It wasn't the traditional white, but a softly clinging flame pink sheath with a side slit and a low neckline tied with a narrow ribbon. Terribly seductive, and even her mother hadn't seen it. A good deal of the bodice was see-through lace, and the side slit was edged with it too. Usually she wore a nightshirt or a cotton shortie nightdress—girlish fashions. When she had seen this and tried it on in the shop it had made her feel every inch a woman. Now she just felt over-exposed, wishing that there was a cover-up of some sort to go with it, but she wasn't the negligée type, she had decided after trying several glamorous robes in the shops. The only thing she had was a short silk kimono, and she had left that in the bedroom. She listened, wondering if Simon was in there.

Hearing nothing, she dropped her undies into the Ali Baba basket by the basin and gathered up her clothes, prepared to whip smartly into the room and find the kimono before he came in.

She had taken three steps when she realised that he was lying in the bed. The cotton cover had been removed and the sheets were turned down. Meredith started. 'Oh! You're here!'

'Well, yes,' he said, raising his brows. 'I'm your husband, remember?'

'I didn't hear you come in.' She went to the wardrobe and hung up her skirt and blouse. At least with her back to him the nightdress wasn't quite so revealing. But eventually she had to turn, going to the dressing table and seating herself on the little cane stool facing it as she picked up her hairbrush.

Simon got off the bed and came to lean on the dressing table, smiling down at her. She looked up and saw his bare, golden-tanned chest, a line of almost invisible fair hair down the middle. She raised her eyes to his face, finding a half smile on his mouth, and something she couldn't read in his eyes. He said softly, 'Now.'

Her heart plummeted in sudden, unreasonable fright. Eyes dilating, she said faintly, 'What?'

The smile deepened. 'Now,' he repeated. 'Undo your hair for me, Meredith.'

'Oh!' she breathed in sheer relief. She put up her hands and began pulling out the pins, slowly because she found his presence inhibiting and her hands were clumsy. She looked in the mirror, unable to meet his eyes, but the mirror showed her own bare shoulders, the swell of her breasts barely covered by the lace trimming of the nightgown, and the silky skin of her inner arms as she raised them. She thought that this was what he could see, and her heart beat erratically. Her skin had a healthy summer tan, but beneath it was a pallor of exhaustion and strain, and faint shadows under eyes which looked dark and huge. She thought she looked plain and terribly young, and wished she had put on some make-up in the bathroom and made herself more attractive and mature-looking.

The last pin dropped on the dressing table, and she shook back her hair and picked up the brush. She managed a dozen or so slow strokes, then put down the hairbrush.

'You're supposed to do a hundred, aren't you?' he asked, and picked up the brush as though offering to carry on.

She shook her head. 'Not tonight, I'm too tired.'

His brows went up, and she thought how gauche and stupid she must sound, saying that to him on their wedding night. She stood up abruptly and he replaced the brush on the dressing table and caught her arm, pulling her into a loose embrace. He lifted her chin with his finger, then traced the blueness under her eyes. 'You are, too,' he said. 'It's been a long day, hasn't it?'

And the most important part is still to come, she thought. She wished she didn't feel so dead. It wasn't just today, it was the weeks of preparation beforehand. All the late nights and hectic days were catching up on her.

He kissed her gently, and she stood passively in his arms, her lips slackly acceptant. His hand ran down her back to the edge of the gorgeous gown, and he folded her closely in his arms and kissed her again, trying to rouse a response which she was totally unable to give. He stopped kissing her and his chest trembled with a breath of laughter. 'You just want to sleep, don't you?'

'Oh no!' she said, her hands going to his bare upper arms. 'I didn't mean that, honestly.'

'Shh, it doesn't matter,' he said. 'Come to bed. The rest will keep.'

He made her get under the sheet and slid in beside her, and she turned to him and put her arms around his neck. With her lips against his shoulder, she said, 'I don't mind, if you want to——' She was shivering with tension and tiredness. 'It'll be all right for you anyway, won't it?'

He took her shoulders and pushed her back on to the pillow. 'No, it won't be all right,' he said firmly. 'What sort of a monster do you think I am? I don't want to enjoy my own pleasure while you suffer in silence.'

'You wouldn't let me suffer,' she said.

He looked at her, saying nothing for a moment. 'No, but I want you to like it—love it. And you can't in the state of exhaustion you're in now. Tomorrow—or the next day—whenever you really want it.'

'Oh, Simon.' She nuzzled into his chest, tears of relief and gratitude trickling on to his skin. 'I'm sorry. It's so unfair for you.'

'I've waited a long time already, Meredith. It isn't going to hurt me to wait a day or two more. There's no law that says a marriage has to be consummated on the wedding night. In fact, it's probably a damned stupid idea. I'm sure you're not the first bride to feel this way. Getting married is a hell of a strain, then there's usually a long journey involved, and at the end of it you're supposed to be all ready for a session of passionate lovemaking. It's unnatural. What you need is a decent rest, and that's what you're going to have. Now stop worrying.'

He held her until she went to sleep, and it didn't take long. The sound of the sea came whispering in through the window, and his arms were an amazingly comfortable resting place.

CHAPTER EIGHT

IN the morning she woke alone, although the place in the bed beside her was still warm, and she could see the indentation of Simon's head on the pillow next to hers.

He came out of the bathroom moments later, wearing blue swim briefs and with a towel in his hand.

'Hello, sleepyhead,' he greeted her. 'How about a swim before breakfast?'

He came to sit on the bed close to her and she sat up, pushing her hair away from her face. The strap of the nightdress slipped as she moved, half exposing her breast, and before she could free her hand from the bedclothes to adjust it, Simon slid his fingers under the narrow ribbon, bent swiftly to plant a fleeting kiss on the curve of warm flesh, and deftly pulled back on to her shoulder.

His hand strayed down her arm. 'Or, we could stay in bed a bit longer,' he said, a question in his voice.

Her heart was thumping and she could still

feel the imprint of his kiss. But she needed to go to the bathroom, and her mouth tasted of the aftermath of yesterday's champagne.

He leaned closer as though intending to kiss her lips, and she ducked her head quickly and said, 'I'd love a swim. Will you wait for me?'

'Of course,' he said, his eyes on her downbent head. 'But not for too long.'

She looked up into his eyes, saw the hidden meaning in his words and said steadily, 'I'll be ready soon. I promise.'

'Good.' He stood up and pulled the bedclothes off her, his eyes sliding down the slim figure under the clinging gown, and the long line of her legs. 'Come on, then, woman. Get a move on.'

In the bathroom she plaited her hair and pinned it out of the way, then put on a black bikini patterned with yellow-centred daisies, and covered that with her kimono.

'Will I need sandals?' she asked Simon, coming back into the bedroom.

'No, I don't think so. It's all grass and sand down to the beach. Have you got a towel?'

She had a big beach towel that she had

unpacked the night before. Simon took it from her and slung his own towel about his neck as they let themselves out into the sunlit morning.

Behind the cottage was a dark mass of bush, the tops of the tallest trees moved by a soft breeze. In front of it tough strands of buffalo grass matted the sand that showed through in pale patches, and on the steep slope to the beach a stand of pines had dropped a slippery carpet of dried brown needles. The horizon was visible between the rough, resinous trunks as they walked, a deep line of indigo separating the pale blue of the sky and the green of the sea.

Simon took her hand as they reached a series of low dunes where furry cat-tails brushed their ankles, and then they were on a wide beach of cream and silver sand, confined by almost identical headlands where old pohutukawas dipped their twisted branches into the sea. The waves coming into shore were crested with white and travelling fast, though not very high.

They left their towels and Meredith's kimono on a driftwood log that lay partly buried in the soft sand, and ran into the water hand in hand, gasping at the first cold shock but soon becoming accustomed to the temperature. They dived into the waves, swam out to smooth water and then back in again, and splashed and chased each other for half an hour.

Racing up the beach, with Simon a few feet behind her, Meredith felt her skin pimpling with gooseflesh, and shivered as she picked up her towel.

Simon took it from her and began to rub her down, against her laughing protest.

'You're cold,' he said.

'Not really. It was lovely.'

He had reached her legs and was briskly drying them, going on one knee on the sand. She looked down at the fair hair darkened with water, sleeked to the shape of his head. His towel was still lying on the log within arm's reach, and she bent sideways and picked it up and began to dry his hair.

He stood up quite suddenly, the towel whipping out of her hands and falling about his neck, and he wrapped hers round her like a sarong and secured it firmly by tucking the end under in front.

Meredith lifted her hands to continue what

she had begun, but he caught them in his and said, 'I'm okay.'

'Fair's fair,' she told him, freeing herself from his loose clasp. She took the towel back and dried his arms and chest. 'Turn around,' she said briskly.

He smiled and put his hands on his narrow hips and presented his back to her.

She rubbed the towel over his firm torso as far as the band of his briefs, then stooped and wiped it down his legs. She sat on her haunches on the sand and said again, 'Turn around.'

Assiduously she started at his ankles, but when she reached his thighs he suddenly bent and hauled her up with his hands under her armpits, 'Meredith, *no!*'

He was smiling grimly, and though she could feel colour in her cheeks, she held his eyes and smiled back and said, 'Why not?'

'You know perfectly well why not!'

'Prude!' she said, her hands on his shoulders, the towel still held in one of them. 'We're married, aren't we?'

'Yes we are,' he said, suddenly sliding his arms about her waist and hauling her close, his hands going lower to hold her intimately against him. 'And later on, little tease, you'll find out just how much of a *prude* I am. Right now, you're cold and I'm hungry. Breakfast.'

He let her go, with a gentle slap on her still damp behind, and picked up her kimono, placing it about her shoulders.

They got dressed and then Meredith made the bed while Simon cooked the bacon and eggs. She rinsed and partially dried her hair, combing the damp tresses out, and put a towel about her shoulders, over the pink blouse she had donned with a washed denim skirt.

'How long does it take to dry?' Simon asked, lightly touching her hair as he put a plate in front of her at the table.

'Oh, a couple of hours if it dries naturally. I have a portable drier, but that isn't good for it. I should really have shampooed it and used a conditioner just now.'

'It must take a lot of looking after.'

'Yes. Sometimes I think I'd rather have it cut.'

'Why don't you?'

'Would you mind?'

'Would *I* mind?' He sounded surprised.

'Yes. I thought you—well, most men like long hair on women, don't they?' Jill had worn her fine blonde hair long, although not as long as Meredith's.

'You're the one who has to wear it. Get it cut if that's what you want.'

'You wouldn't be—disappointed?'

'No. I don't mind one way or the other. It looks very nice, but if it's a hassle, why bother? I didn't marry you for your hair.'

He was cutting into his egg, and she bent her gaze to her own plate and picked up her knife and fork. He sounded as though it didn't matter a bit. Michael had said once that long hair was sexy, and that most men preferred it. Francine's was short, but maybe she would grow it for him. She couldn't help wondering if Simon would have minded if Jill had cut her hair.

To take her mind off that train of thought, she said to him, 'You're a good cook.' The bacon was crisp and not overdone, the eggs still soft, the yolks overlaid with a milky skin.

'I've had plenty of practise,' he commented. 'But tomorrow it's your turn.'

'I make a great omelette,' she boasted.

'Omelettes it is, then,' he said easily. 'I'll look forward to it. What do you want to do today?'

'Laze,' she said. 'Explore. A bit of both. The sun's warming up now. I could sit outside and dry my hair after breakfast.'

'After you've done the dishes.'

'Yes, oh lord and master,' she mocked him. 'But if I cook tomorrow, *you* get to do the dishes.'

'Of course,' he agreed.

'And make the bed.'

He looked up, quizzing her aggressive tone. 'Okay,' he acknowledged. 'I can do that, too.'

His father wouldn't have, she knew. The division of labour in the Van Dyk household had always been strictly by sex. The boys worked out on the farm with their father, and the girls and Mrs Van Dyk were responsible for the house. Meredith didn't know if Simon's competence at household tasks was the result of Jill's training or the fact that he had been of necessity fending for himself since her death.

'Meredith,' he said, breaking into her thoughts, 'you did go to the clinic, didn't you?'

'What?' She looked up, startled, and then realised what he meant. 'I went to my own doctor,' she said. 'He gave me some pills. I've already been taking them.'

'No problems?'

'For the first couple of days I felt a bit sick, but I've got over that now. It's what they call a mini-pill, and the doctor said it has fewer side effects than the stronger sort, and that if there are some they usually pass off quite quickly.'

'Is it reliable?'

'Oh, yes. Provided I take it every day at about the same time.'

'Better be sure you do, then.'

Meredith was slightly nettled at his tone. She wasn't a child, or irresponsible, and she hadn't specially wanted to use any birth control method, anyway. She finished her bacon and egg and he pushed the butter over as she took a piece of toast. 'Marmalade?'

'No, thanks.' She shook her head, adding, 'You should have put that in a jam dish. Your mother would never stand for a tin of marmalade on the table.'

'My mother isn't here,' he said. 'Does it offend your sensibilities?'

It didn't, but she had felt an obscure need to hit back at him a little, even with a minor criticism. Ashamed of herself, she shook her head again silently, concentrating on cutting her piece of toast into squares.

'What have I done, Meredith?' he asked mildly.

'Nothing.'

'Go on. I can feel the ice from here.'

'Nothing.' She glanced up, her eyes angry, and saw his questioning, sceptical smile. 'You were being bossy,' she said finally.

'Was I?'

'Yes.'

He looked considering. 'Are you trying to start a quarrel?'

'No, I'm not! Only you can't start bullying me just because we're married.'

'My darling, I have no such intention, believe me.' He put a hand across the table and caught her fingers in his. 'Have I ever been a bully?'

Her simmering annoyance disappeared in a wave of compunction. 'No, of course not,' she admitted. 'I'm sorry. I didn't mean it.'

'I know you didn't,' he said, 'and I didn't mean to be overbearing. Come on, eat your toast. Do you want something else on it instead of marmalade?'

'No thanks. I like it with just butter.'

'Don't you ever eat marmalade?'

She shook her head, taking a bite of her toast. 'Hate it,' she mumbled.

'I've known you all your life,' he said, 'and I never knew that.'

Meredith swallowed. 'There's a lot you don't know about me,' she said, bridling. He needn't think she was an open book just because they had lived practically next door for ever. There was an awful lot about him that she didn't know, too. Some of it she would never know, she realised with a hollow feeling in her stomach. The years he had been married to Jill would always be something she could have no share in, something private and intimate that she couldn't even ask about.

It was a depressing thought, and she firmly pushed it aside. They had all the future together, didn't they, to build memories and intimate moments of their own? It was morbid to dwell in the past. Simon didn't do it, and there was absolutely no point in her doing so.

She brushed her hair dry in the sun, and afterwards they went for a stroll in the bush, their feet making hardly a sound on the spongy carpet of fallen leaves, so that they scarcely disturbed the wood pigeons and tuis and fantails that inhabited the tall trees. Loops of lianas swung down to ground level from some of the highest branches, and tiny-leaved creepers with tough, wire-like stems crawled over the mossy, decaying trunks of giant trees that had fallen long ago.

'I didn't think there was any real bush left in this part of the country,' Meredith said, 'after all those bare paddocks we came through last night!'

'Mm, it's sheep country,' Simon said. 'But fortunately the farmer here decided to preserve this little patch.' He stooped to pick up a brilliant cerise feather. 'Look at this.'

'Gorgeous! A pigeon's, I suppose.'

'Want to keep it?'

'Yes.' She took it from him and slipped it into the pocket of her skirt. 'I'd love a nikau bowl, do you think we could find one?'

'Probably. There are nikau palms here. There?' He pointed, spotting one of the large, distinctive bowl-shaped appendages at the trunk end of a palm leaf that had fallen from its parent tree.

They picked it up, but found it had split badly. Disappointed, Meredith discarded it. 'But there must be some good ones.'

They found two in the end, and she bore them back triumphantly to the bach, placing them on the table. 'This one,' she said, indicating the one with about a foot of thick stem attached, 'can hang on the wall. And the other one I'll varnish and use for a fruit bowl on the kitchen table. They'll be just right in your—our house.' Suddenly anxious, she said, 'You do like them, don't you?'

'I'm sure you'll make them look a million dollars,' he said, smiling.

Meredith grimaced. 'Well, maybe not quite, but cleaned up and with a coat of clear satin finish they'll look terrific, I promise you.'

'I believe you. Right now, though, how about some lunch? It's nearly two o'clock.'

'I've known you all my life,' she said solemnly, paraphrasing his remark of that morning, 'and I never knew that all you think about is your stomach!'

He advanced towards her with a purposeful expression, and she backed, laughing, trying without success to ward him off with her hands. He caught her to him and kissed her, bending her dramatically over his arm like a twenties film heroine, and exploring her lips unmercifully until she could do nothing but wind her arms about his neck and kiss him back.

'Now,' he said when at last he allowed her up for air, 'what was that you said?'

'I take it back!' she panted, gasping for breath. 'I take it all back!'

'I should think so,' he grunted, releasing her. 'But first things first. Now, where's my dinner?'

'Yes, sir, coming, sir, right away, sir,' she babbled, retreating to the kitchen. He came after her, mock-threatening, and cornered her by the sink and kissed her again, and she parted her lips and clutched at his shoulders as sparks of delight shot through her.

They stood there for a long time, and when his arms loosened at last she was flushed and bright-eyed. Her voice husky, she said, 'What do you want for lunch?'

He rubbed his cheek against hers and said, 'Anything. Sandwiches will do. We've got some white wine. Shall I open it?'

'Mmm, yes,' she said, reluctantly moving away from him. 'Wine with tomato and cucumber and cream cheese sandwiches—it sounds deliciously decadent.'

'What would you know about decadence?' he scoffed, opening the small refrigerator.

She made a face at him and flipped up the top of the bread bin.

After lunch they changed again into swim wear and took two glasses and the remains of the wine down to the beach. Simon spread a blanket on the sand and put their beach towels on top of it, then poured wine into the glasses, handing her one as she subsided on to her towel.

He rested on one elbow, watching the sea and sipping at his glass, while Meredith sat with her legs curled to one side. The green of the morning sea had given way to a deep, intense blue except where the breakers curled lazily and persistently in towards the shore. Gulls wheeled occasionally overhead, distantly squawking, and a couple of long-beaked oystercatchers patrolled the water's edge.

Simon finished his drink, put the glass alongside the bottle in the basket they had brought down with them, and lay back, his head resting on his hands, his long legs stretched out.

When Meredith had drained her glass, he put out his hand to take it from her and put it away. Lifting a bottle of suntan lotion from the basket he said, 'Did you use a sunscreen before we came out?'

She nodded. 'Yes, I did. I'm all right.' She lay down, watching him rub the cream over his chest and legs. His skin was basically fair, liable to burn, and he tanned slowly and lightly, whereas she browned in summer with no trouble at all.

'Do my back for me?' he asked her, handing her the bottle. He turned on his face and she smoothed the cool liquid over his skin.

She put a little on her own face and neck as an extra precaution, then left the bottle on a corner of her towel and lay prone, reaching behind her to undo the top of her bikini.

They sunbathed in silence for some time, until she turned on to her back, holding the bra with one hand, and then fumbled with the knot behind her neck to untie the halter strap.

Simon had moved too, sitting up with one forearm resting on his raised knees. 'Why don't you take it off?' he asked.

'What?' She looked up at him, startled.

'I'm the only one here to see,' he said. 'It's a private beach and we have it all to ourselves.'

'Don't the farmer and his family use it?'

'No. They swim further round, apparently. This little piece goes with the cottage.'

'I don't know,' she said doubtfully, and he laughed and leaned over her to whisper in her ear, 'Who's the prude now?'

She pushed at him, and the top, loosely draped across her breasts, slipped. She grabbed it, met his teasing eyes, and almost defiantly discarded it on the sand.

His glance seemed quite dispassionate as he looked at her. 'You'll need some lotion there,' he said, reaching across her for it.

Meredith closed her yes, shivering in anticipation even before the cold moisture touched her skin. His hands soon warmed it, massaging the soft curves with slow, erotic movements. She tried to pretend an indifference she couldn't feel, embarrassed that her body was clearly betraying her response to his touch. He was enjoying it, too, his fingers caressing her knowingly before he withdrew his hands and moved away from her. Unable to bear the tension, to handle the multiple sensations he had aroused, she flipped over again on her stomach, hiding her hot face against her arms and trying to steady her breathing. She thought she heard a breath of laughter from Simon, but he didn't touch her again and after a long while she dozed off in the sun.

Simon's hand on her shoulder woke her. 'Hey,' he said, 'you've been snoozing long enough. How about a swim?'

She murmured protestingly and rolled over before she recalled her missing top. But his eyes stayed unwaveringly on her face as he said, 'You could get sunstroke lying around here all day, you know. Come on, lazy.'

He grabbed her hand and pulled her up, but she hung back. 'Wait, Simon, I can't go in topless!'

'Why not?' he said, glancing down at her bare breasts. 'I am.'

It was no good telling him that that was different, he knew it anyway, and his eyes were laughing at her, daring her to say it.

Well, why not? As he had said, they had the beach to themselves, and the halter pulled uncomfortably at the back of her neck when she wore it in the water. He was hardly even looking at her, and he was her husband, for heaven's sake. She'd have to get used to being more than half-naked with him sometime. Suddenly losing her self-consciousness, she shrugged resignedly and let him lead her into the water. The feeling of freedom was fantastic, and when they came out she collapsed on her stomach, panting, and let the sun dry the salt water on her skin while Simon lay beside her, giving her smiling glances as they talked in a desultory way. After a while he reached for the bottle of suntan lotion, and began smoothing it over her body. He took his time, and she closed her eyes, passively enjoying the sensuousness of his touch, the heat of the sun on her skin adding to the slow erotic fever that was building in her.

Even when he stopped, the feelings didn't entirely subside. She knew he was close beside her and there was an exquisite tension in wondering when he would next touch her, and how. Once or twice he trailed a long finger along her arm or her leg; and once, when she turned over on to her back, he put some more cream on her breasts and when he had finished, gently kissed them and nibbled at her briefly with his lips, making her ache with desire. Then he moved away, his arm across her and his hand resting on her hip the only contact between them. It was a gradual, step-by-step seduction, and she didn't want to hurry any part of it in spite of the increasingly urgent messages her body was conveying to his.

The afternoon waned, and as the sun disappeared beyond the pine plantation, the shadows of the trees almost touched the beach. Meredith shivered, and Simon rubbed her arm lightly. 'Cold?'

The sand was still quite warm, but the heat of the sun was fading. 'I will be soon,' she said regretfully.

He shifted until he was poised over her, his thigh against hers. 'I'll warm you up,' he said, and she smiled back at him, her body already inflamed by his touch.

His eyes studied her face and then her breasts, lingering there appreciatively before they passed on with deliberation to the rest of her body. 'You're very beautiful, Meredith,' he said. 'I want to make love to you—very much.'

'I want you to,' she whispered, meeting his eyes as they returned to her face.

Simon smiled, something like triumph leaping in his eyes. He bent his head and kissed her sweetly, exploratively, and his hand lightly skimmed from her shoulder to her knee, returning to her waist, then cupping one sun-warmed breast. Meredith's hands were on his shoulders, her mouth opening under his. His other hand slid under her, bringing their bodies into closer contact, and the beach, the sky, the world receded as a singing pleasure took hold of her, building to a higher and higher pitch. She had never felt like this before, almost out of control, wanting to beg him to keep touching her, kissing her, and never stop. With Michael she had experienced stirrings of desire, of sexual need, but she had always been able to control them. This was utterly different.

Simon moved until they were on their sides, locked together, and then, still holding her tightly, rolled on to his back so that she was lying above and across him, one leg between his lifted thighs. The pleasure was so intense that she broke the kiss in some sort of bewilderment and dropped her forehead against his naked shoulder with a small sound that was almost a whimper.

He changed their position again, laying her back against the blanket so that he could see her face. 'Are you all right?' he asked her, his hand smoothing her cheek, slightly roughened with grains of sand.

She nodded. 'I like it so much,' she confessed, 'I don't think I can bear it.'

He laughed softly. 'We haven't even started yet.' He ran his hand up her inner thigh, and she gasped and choked out, 'Oh, Simon!'

'You're a very sexy lady,' he commented.

Her face flaming, she said, 'I'm not! Well, if I am it's your doing!'

'And I love the way you respond to me,' he said, his voice deep and not quite steady. 'Only this isn't really the most comfortable place for your first time. We'll go back to the house.'

CHAPTER NINE

SHE woke at dusk, her cheek on Simon's bare shoulder, her hair fanned across his chest. His arm was still curled about her, and she could feel the length of his leg against hers.

He turned his head and looked at her through half-closed eyes, and she said, 'Is your arm asleep?'

'No.' His lips feathered a kiss across her brow. 'I'm perfectly comfortable. You?'

'Mmm,' she murmured, snuggling down a little further in the bed. 'Blissful.'

It had been all she could ever have wished for. Simon had paced his passion to hers, prepared to be infinitely patient and careful, and she knew she owed her own enjoyment to that care, because he had managed not to hurt her at all. She had felt only mounting delight and a blinding starburst of fulfilment at the last. She had loved every minute of it, as he had told her he wanted her to, and she knew she had delighted him, too, that her intense, flagrant pleasure had added to his own.

His hand stroked her back, and his lips moved down to hers, capturing them in a long, lazy, drugging kiss. Tiny waves of lovely sensation began rippling through her body, and her breathing quickened. She lifted her knee and let her thigh rest across his, and his involuntary reaction evoked a thrill of pure joy. His other arm came round her, dragging her even closer, and for a moment she hesitated, almost afraid that nothing could be as good as the first time, not wanting to spoil it. But he wasn't going to stop now, and this time there was no holding back, her desire soon matched his and he knew it. He took her with sweet violence, and she wanted that, wanted his male strength, his uncontrolled passion, the tacit confession that he found her irresistible, that she could make him forget everything except a frantic need to slake himself on her body. The force of his sensuality no longer had the power to frighten her, since she had discovered an equal force in herself.

Later they got up, washed, and had a meal, and then Meredith put on the beautiful nightdress again, and brushed her hair until it shone while Simon watched, lounging on the bed. She stood before him and carefully tied the ribbons on the front of the flame-red gown into a neat bow. He smiled, and she smiled back at him. They both knew that she was wearing the nightdress for the sheer pleasure it would give him to take it off.

The days and nights of their honeymoon merged into one another like a single golden dream. They made love often, in the daytime as well as during the night, and sometimes they swam at night and strolled along the beach naked in the moonlight and made love again on the soft, dry sand. 'You're amazing,' Simon told her. 'You seemed so shy I thought I'd have to be terribly careful with you, take things slowly so as not to shock you too much.'

Was that how it had been with Jill? she wondered. Impossible to ask, of course, and pointless thinking of it. She was pretty sure that Jill, too, had been a virgin bride.

'I'm greedy,' she said, banishing the thought. 'I want everything all at once. You know I've always been like that.'

'I know you've always gone hell for leather at anything you do,' he admitted, smiling.

'And you have a very stubborn will when you want something. Your enthusiasm did need curbing when you were young.'

'Do you want me to curb my enthusiasm now?' she challenged him. Her hand had been playing lightly over his chest, her nails drawing invisible patterns from his navel to his collar bone.

'No,' he said as she leaned over to flick her tongue into the hollow at the base of his throat, splaying her hand over his heart. 'Not when it leads you to——' he gasped and groaned as she moved closer, rubbing against him and letting her fingers stray further down, '—to do *that*! God, darling, you know what it does to me!'

'I know,' she said, mock-demure, her tongue briefly appearing between her teeth. 'And I like it.'

Sometimes she wondered if she could have lost her shyness as quickly with him, and been as ready to acknowledge her own sensuality, if she had not known him so well in other ways. The closeness they shared was in a way only an extension of a less sexually aware closeness that had been growing and deepening all her life.

By the time they had to return to the real world and the everyday, she knew she was fathoms deep in love with her husband, that Michael had never mattered half as much as she had imagined, and that everything she had ever felt for him was not even the palest shadow of the emotion that Simon aroused in her.

They slipped into their new routine quietly enough on the surface. Meredith had some savings which she enjoyed spending on refurbishing the house and expressing some of her own taste. She was careful to consult Simon before getting rid of anything that he might have a sentimental attachment to, but for the most part he went along with her alterations and additions, and she thought the place had begun to seem more homely.

They had bought a bed together during their engagement, a wide one with extra length to accommodate Simon's long legs. The bedhead and footboard were attractively grained rimu with inset panels of latticework cane. She had never been in his bedroom and didn't know what the bed replaced—the one he had shared with Jill or a single bed that he might have bought for himself when he moved to Whangarei.

The chest of drawers that Simon used for his clothes was not new, but it was rimu too, and they bought a matching dressing table with drawers for Meredith and placed it next to the built-in wardrobe. It had occurred to Meredith that there was no photograph of Jill in the house, but one day when she opened a drawer to put away some clothes of Simon's, she found it nearly empty, and at the bottom was a framed picture, face down.

She knew immediately what it was, but couldn't resist picking it up and turning it over in her hands. Jill's face smiled up at her, and with extraordinary suddenness, Meredith felt a terrible shaft of pain and grief—for Jill, for the loss that Simon had suffered, and, inexplicably, for herself. She sat down on the bed, still holding the picture, and wept uncontrollably.

When it was over, and she had scrabbled for some tissues in the drawer of her bedside table and blown her nose, she thought how ridiculous that had been. She and Simon were happy—she loved him and she knew he loved her, although she had no way of knowing how his feelings for her compared with what he had shared with Jill. It was tragic that Jill had died, but it wasn't Simon's fault or Meredith's. And she was sure that Jill would have liked to know that Simon had achieved happiness of whatever sort with someone else.

She put away the photograph just as she had found it, wondering if Simon ever took it out and looked at it when he was alone. Better not to speculate on that. In the bathroom she rinsed her eyes with cold water and put on some make-up to hide the traces of her tears, and brushed back her hair from her eyes. She would have it cut, she decided. It made her look too young, anyway, and soon Benjy would be coming to live with them. She was going to be his mother, albeit a surrogate one. She ought to try to look a bit more mature. They didn't have any intention of making a secret of his parentage, but she didn't want to have to explain to every casual stranger that, although she was actually old enough to be Benjy's natural mother, she hadn't in fact given birth to him.

She went to a hairdresser and emerged with her hair shortened so that the ends, gently turned under, lay on her nape, almost touching her shoulders. It felt light and free, and she had an urge to keep shaking her head so that the soft strands swung against her jawline.

'Very nice,' Simon commented that evening when he arrived home and she greeted him self-consciously at the door. 'How does it feel?'

'Terrific,' she said. 'I can't think why I didn't do it before.'

'Shall we have dinner in town so that you can show it off?' he suggested. 'We won't have so many chances to go out once Ben comes to live with us.'

She had thawed a couple of chops and peeled some potatoes, but the potatoes could be eaten fried tomorrow, and the steak would keep in the refrigerator until tomorrow. 'Yes,' she said, 'I'd like that.'

Over dinner she fingered her hair and said, 'Does it make me look any older, do you think?'

Simon shook his head. 'A little more worldly, perhaps.'

'Worldly?' she tried out the word, wrinkling her nose. 'You mean sophisticated?'

'I suppose so. Why—was that the object of the exercise?'

'Sort of. I thought I should try and look like a mother when Benjy comes.'

He laughed. 'You look beautiful, and that's all that matters.'

She grinned at him. 'I still haven't got used to receiving compliments from you.'

'Nonsense, I distinctly remember when you were only a kid telling you that you had a good, logical mind.'

'Oh, that!'

'What do you mean, "Oh that!" At the time you were dead chuffed, you even blushed.'

'That was because you kissed me,' she informed him. Not that she hadn't relished the compliment. His praise had thrilled her at least as much as the kiss.

'Did I?' He looked surprised and enquiring.

'*Simon!*' she wailed indignantly, knowing the laughter in her eyes gave her away. 'You mean you've forgotten our very first kiss?'

'Sorry, my love,' he said, unrepentant. 'But at fourteen you weren't the luscious female you are now. And school uniforms might turn some men on, but aren't you lucky I'm not kinky that way?'

She choked on her soufflé. 'Oh, you! You always manage to twist an argument to your own advantage.' In the area of logical thinking he was still streets ahead of her, although he had taught her a lot. 'Anyway, that wasn't the kind of compliment I was talking about.'

'I thought it was the only kind a woman deemed worth having in these liberated times.'

'Hah! Shows how much you know about women!'

His eyes were laughing at her. 'I'm only interested in one, and I know a fair bit about you.' He lowered his voice to a seductive murmur. 'For instance, if I want to drive you wild in bed, all I need to do——'

'*Simon!*' she hissed, terrified that someone would overhear. 'Stop it!'

'You don't say that when I——'

'*Simon!*'

He grinned wickedly, and she succumbed to a fit of giggles. 'Beast!' she said when they had subsided. 'Don't *say* things like that to me in public!'

'Let's go home and I'll say them all again in private,' he suggested.

'I haven't had my pudding yet!'

'And didn't you once accuse *me* of thinking only of my stomach?'

'As I remember, you had a very effective answer for that.'

'Go on then,' he dared her. 'I won't mind.'

'We'd get thrown out.'

'Chicken!'

She leaned over the table and kissed him very briefly. 'There!'

'Okay, that'll do for now,' he said grudgingly. 'But you'd better make a proper job of it later.'

They smiled at each other, their eyes flirting, daring, promising, and she thought, it's perfect, it's all perfect. I love him so much and I'm sure he loves me. He can't go on loving a dead girl more than the one who's sharing his bed, his life—even, pretty soon, his son!

Attending Michael's wedding, an event she had dreaded so short a time ago, was no problem at all. She noticed, with a trace of amusement, that Francine's curls now brushed her shoulders, and that Michael stared hard at her own shorter hairstyle as she kissed him lightly and wished him well with the utmost sincerity. They went to the Kingsley's house after the reception and waved the happy couple on their way to their honeymoon, and later as Simon drove home, he took her hand in his and glanced at her with a hint of anxiety and said, 'Okay?'

'Everything's okay,' she told him quite firmly, and leaned over to kiss his cheek, a subtle reinforcement.

He gave her a more searching look, then raised her fingers to his lips before releasing her hand to change gear. That night he made love to her with a peculiarly attentive passion, and held her afterwards so that she went to sleep in his arms.

They collected Benjy on a Friday night so that Simon could spend the whole weekend with him. Already some of his clothes and toys had been moved to the house, and he had helped Meredith buy the material for a new printed cover for his bed. He was accustomed to spending weekends with his father and Meredith, and she hoped that he understood that now he would be living with them on a permanent basis. In six months he would be starting school. By then he should have settled in thoroughly. There was a place waiting for him at the local playcentre for those months, and she hoped he would meet children there who would move on to the same school at about the same time.

'He will be fine,' Simon's mother said as Simon and Benjy carried the child's bags to the car. 'I'm sad to see him go, but it's right. He should be with his father, and a young mother, not an old *oma* like me.'

'You're not old!' Meredith scoffed. Mrs Van Dyk might have had a full life, in many ways a hard one, but she had unlined skin and clear blue eyes, and a zest that was missing in many younger people.

'I'm not young any more. That Benjy can be a mischief, you watch him, Meredith.'

'I will. And we'll bring him to see you often, you know that.'

'Meredith——'

'Yes?'

'You know the picture of Jill that Benjy has—it's always been in his room here.'

'Yes.' She hadn't noticed it lately, though she had been in and out of Benjy's room often enough. It was a small picture in an oval frame, and in the clutter of toys and minor treasures on his dressing table it hadn't stood out particularly, its very familiarity making it almost invisible.

'He wanted to take it with him. Simon has often talked of his mother, you know.'

'Yes. Of course he must have it. It will help him to feel at home.'

'You don't mind, then?'

Meredith shook her head. How could she mind? 'I want Benjy to be happy.'

'You're a good girl, Meredith. I know he will be happy with you—as Simon is happy. It's good to see him really laugh again.'

'Thank you.' Impulsively, Meredith kissed the older woman's smooth, rounded cheek, warmed by her assessment of her son's marriage.

Benjy came running up to kiss his Oma too, with Simon behind him asking Meredith, 'Are you ready to go?' And in a few minutes they were on their way.

Benjy had been promised hamburgers and chips at McDonald's to celebrate the change in his life, and they stopped for that and then drove home.

Meredith unpacked his things while Simon

supervised his bath, and as she was turning down the bed they came into the room, Simon piggybacking Benjy.

'There you are, young son!' he said, dumping the squealing child on the bed. 'In you go.'

Benjy wriggled under the covers, then said virtuously, 'Prayers first!'

'Say them there,' Simon ordered, and Benjy, propped against the bedhead, closed his eyes tightly, folded his hands and whispered fervently for a few minutes.

Simon's eyes wandered to the low, square table by the bed on which Meredith had placed Benjy's favourite teddy bear, several story books, and the photograph of his mother.

She saw Simon's eyes light on the small picture, then he looked at her and questioningly raised his brows. She smiled at him, and he put out his hand and caught one of hers in a firm, warm clasp.

'Finished!' Benjy announced. 'Can I have a story?'

'Sure you can.' Simon sat on the bed, pulling Meredith down beside him. 'What about this one?' He picked up the top book from the pile on the table.

'No. This one.' Benjy leaned over and pulled out one of the others. Simon had to let go of Meredith's hand to read it, but she stayed until the story was finished, and they both kissed Benjy good night before Simon switched off the light, waiting at the door for Meredith to join him.

They were barely in the dim passageway before he caught her to him, holding her tightly. 'I love you,' he whispered, and kissed her almost fiercely, compelling her lips apart, bending her head back with the force of his mouth.

'Let's go to bed,' he said a few moments later. 'I want you.'

They didn't turn on any lights. She let him lead her in the darkness and push her down on the bed, and within minutes they were naked in each other's arms.

Having a lively four-year-old in the house was fun, but tiring. She took him along to the playcentre and was soon involved in its activities, interested enough to start the study course for a preliminary certificate in under-standing children's play and its effect on development, and both she and Benjy made new friends. Some of the mothers were just about her own age, and now that she had a child to look after, her interests had broadened to coincide with theirs. She was invited along to lunch once or twice while Benjy played with other children he had met at the centre, and she began to reciprocate, and to get accustomed to having three or four noisy youngsters whooping through the house and having to be shooed outside periodically to allow the adults to talk.

Some of the women had younger children as well, and Meredith was always willing to hold or feed a baby, or even get in some practise at changing a nappy. She was teased about being 'clucky', and one or two of the young mothers assumed that before long she would be starting a baby of her own.

She thought that with Benjy starting school in a few months, it might be worth broaching the subject with Simon again. But when she suggested one evening after Benjy had gone to bed that she might stop taking her pills, he brought her up short with an uncompromising veto.

'But you said about a year,' she reminded

him.

'I said we'd talk about it again. And it's not even close to a year.'

'It would be more by the time the baby's born. It takes nine months, you know. And I might not get pregnant right away.'

'I know how long it takes, Meredith,' he said sarcastically. 'And I don't want you pregnant when Ben's just starting school. It's a big step in a child's life, especially after the changes he's had this year, and it would hardly be the best time to start another family.'

'I think it would be an ideal time! If you mean he'd feel supplanted or something, I don't think we need worry about that. It would be four or five months before we'd have to tell him about it, and he'd be well settled at school by then.'

'I'm sorry, I don't agree.' There was finality in his voice and his face.

She looked down at her hands, her mouth tight.

He came to sit beside her on the sofa, his hand going over hers. 'I know you love babies and you want a family,' he said, 'but we've been married for less than half a year.

I'm just suggesting that we wait a little longer.'

'How much longer?' She raised her head and looked fully into his eyes.

He smiled slightly. 'Do we have to have it cut and dried? Don't be so impatient, darling. You've got Ben to look after, and I can see you're pretty tired sometimes.' He placed a finger on her lips as she made to protest. 'I know you enjoy it, but the fact remains that even Ben is quite a handful. Being pregnant will make you still more tired, and possibly quite sick for a while. It isn't all roses.'

'I know that!' she snapped, 'but I'm prepared to put up with it, and morning sickness doesn't go on forever.'

'Still, it's unpleasant while it lasts. Maybe when Ben's got used to going to school—and you'll be a bit more rested, having him away all day.'

'He'll be older,' she reminded him. 'It will make a bigger gap between him and the next one. Don't you think he should have a younger sister or brother as soon as possible?'

'I didn't marry you to turn you into a baby mill for my son's benefit.'

'I thought you wanted him to have a proper

family.'

'I do, you know that. Only there's no reason to rush into having a family quite so soon. Most people prefer to wait a little while and let their marriage consolidate first. It's not a bad idea, you know.'

'Our marriage is all right, isn't it?' she asked with a stirring of anxiety. 'We knew each other so well before. It doesn't seem necessary in our case.'

'Don't you think so?' He smiled. 'I'm discovering new things about you all the time. We didn't have very much time to get used to being married before Ben came to us. It's quite an adjustment for both of you.'

'I manage him all right. I know that lately he's been a bit less obedient, and we've had a couple of tussles of will, but I think that's a good sign. He's accepted me as someone normal in his life, not just a sort of visitor that he puts on his best behaviour for.'

'You're probably right, but don't you think that you've got enough on your plate, just now?'

'I want a baby, Simon. I'm sure it would be all right. Surely I ought to know what I can cope with? I wouldn't even be taking the pill if you hadn't insisted. I've always wanted children of my own.'

He said slowly, 'You know, I could be hurt—you didn't marry me simply to have a legal reason for getting pregnant, did you?'

'Of course I didn't!' She pulled her hands away from his. 'That's a horrible thing to say!'

'All right,' he said. 'But you're making me feel as though giving you babies is my ultimate function.'

'I don't mean to!' She didn't know how he could have thought so, but perhaps to a man it might seem like that. It wasn't just that she wanted a baby—she wanted *his* baby, the outcome of their love for each other, a new person made out of that love. 'Oh, you can't seriously think that!' she said, half annoyed with him.

He shrugged rather coldly. 'What's more important to you, our marriage or your longing for a baby?'

'That isn't fair!' she protested. 'If we have children they'll be part of our marriage. It isn't a question of choice!'

'No,' he agreed. 'It's a question of timing. Let's just wait until we both feel the time's right, shall we?'

Defeated, she had to give in, but the conversation left her feeling confused and upset. Perhaps it was only that her longing for a baby had been frustrated, although Simon had assured her that the frustration would be temporary. His concern for her was genuine, she knew, and his arguments had been quite cogent ones, although she didn't agree with them, and felt that he was making too much of the possible effects of pregnancy on her ability to handle Benjamin.

Perhaps it was true that she was being too impatient, too anxious, as usual, to have everything at once. She knew it was a failing of hers. The one thing she had ever been prepared to wait patiently for was marriage to Michael, and that was only because she had known he had to finish his degree before they could have a home, and she had realised that foisting on him the responsibility of a wife and possibly a family would have interfered with his studies.

Simon wasn't going to be budged, anyway, so she would have to put up with his decision. It was true that most people waited at least a year or two before starting their families, unless, of course, there was already one on the way before the wedding. Benjy had not been born until Simon and Jill had been married for some years. Jill, a teacher, had taken relieving positions during their marriage. Meredith was a little hazy on the details now, but probably she had not even stopped working until she became pregnant. It was the norm, these days.

One thing she was certain of, a baby had to be welcomed by both parents. She must try to accept philosophically that however ready she felt, Simon didn't feel the same. Men often didn't have the strong instinct for parenthood that many women possessed. And he was already a father, as he had once pointedly reminded her. She would just have to wait for what he saw as a reasonable time. Eventually, as he had promised, they would have their family, brothers and sisters for Benjy, babies of her own.

CHAPTER TEN

MEREDITH got on well with Benjy, but in winter when the days were cold and wet she found it quite hard to keep him occupied when it was not a playcentre day. He was an active child, and quiet pursuits like painting and puzzles and books, or even watching television, palled for him quite quickly.

She provided him with playmates as often as possible, and when all else failed played with him herself, helping him to build things with an enormous set of interlocking plastic blocks which the Van Dyks had imported piecemeal over many years from the Netherlands, or taking whatever part he wanted in some elaborate and usually highly physical game of make-believe. Mostly it was fun, but there were times when she tried to gently channel him into doing something on his own for a while so that she could recoup her own resources.

There came a very trying week or two when an epidemic of German measles broke out among the playcentre children, and he

203

succumbed to it. When he became unduly fractious beforehand, Meredith managed to remain patient, realising he was probably getting the disease, and during the few days that he was really sick she devoted all her time and energy to nursing him and keeping his mind off his misery with new games and books and indoor activities. It hit him much harder than she would have expected, and he remained irritable and easily tired even after he returned to the playcentre.

'He'll get over it,' Simon asserted, when she suggested that he might need some sort of tonic, and perhaps she should ask the doctor's opinion. 'He's not sick now, just a bit pulled down. Maybe he should go back to having an afternoon nap for a while.'

'You try and make him!' she said feelingly. She had suggested it once or twice to Benjy, and the resultant battle was definitely not worth the effort it took to make him stay in bed for an hour.

'You're looking a bit pulled down yourself,' Simon remarked. 'You've been immunised, haven't you?'

'Yes, of course,' she said. She had had her immunity checked by her doctor before they got married. 'Not that it would matter,' she couldn't help adding a little bitterly, 'since I'm not allowed to get pregnant, anyway.'

Simon's mouth tightened. 'You're tired,' he said, evading the implied accusation. 'Go and have a rest, and I'll put Ben to bed.'

She still felt tired and a little cross the next day. She took Benjy to the playcentre, and as it wasn't her day for duty, decided to go to Whangarei for the morning, buy some material and start sewing a new dress. Looking in the bargain bin at one of the fabric shops she picked out a piece of wine-red velvet, imagining the effect of the material trimmed with gold buttons and a plain gold leather belt. A remnant of striped brown-and-white material caught her eye, and she thought she could make a shirt for Benjy out of it. A darker brown piece of heavy synthetic would do for a pair of trousers to go with it. She hadn't made boys' things before, it would be a challenge. Perhaps it would cheer them both up.

Benjy was at first intrigued at the idea, looking solemnly at the picture of the little boy on the cover of the pattern she had bought. But he wriggled as she tried the

pieces against him, and soon lost interest
when she began cutting the material on the
kitchen table while he sat on one of the
chairs, swinging his legs.

'Can we go and see Oma and Opa?' he
asked, as she put the scissors down and
removed the pattern pieces.

They had seen his grandparents at the
weekend, and this was only Tuesday. 'Maybe
tomorrow,' she said, folding a flimsy piece of
tissue.

He picked up the scissors, and she said
automatically, 'Put those back, Benjy.'

Benjy ignored her, and she leaned over and
took them from him firmly. His mouth turned
down, and he began to kick the table leg with
his shoes.

'Don't do that,' Meredith said. She placed
the scissors out of his reach and picked up
the pieces of material.

'Want to go to Oma's,' Benjy said sulkily.
He stopped kicking the table and reached for
the scissors.

'No!' Meredith said sharply, pushing his
hand away. 'Those scissors are too big and
sharp for you. If you like you can get the
toybox scissors, and I'll find you some

pictures to cut out.'

'Don't want to.' He started kicking the table again. 'Want to go to Oma's.'

'Benjy, I said don't do that. You'll spoil the table.'

He set his mouth and kicked harder, until she put down the pieces of fabric in her hand and bodily removed him. '*I want to go to Oma's!*' he yelled, his face red with temper. 'I want Oma!'

'*No!*' Meredith shouted back, her patience snapping. More quietly but with some force, she added, 'We are *not* going to Oma's today, I'm busy. And if you don't behave I won't take you to see her tomorrow, either. You can watch me make your shirt, and if you're a good boy, you might be able to wear it tomorrow and show it to Oma and Opa.'

'Don't *want* to!' he stormed. 'Dumb shirt, anyway. I want to see Oma today!'

'Well, you're not,' Meredith said shortly. 'Now go outside or into your room and find something to play with. And please don't bother me!'

He threw her a look of pure hatred, and rushed outside. It was a quite mild winter's day, and he had a jersey on. She glanced out

of the window before she took the sewing
into the other room, and saw him sitting on
the low wooden seat at the edge of his
sandpit, scuffing up sand in an angry way
with his feet. He would get over it, she
thought. He had a fierce temper, but it never
lasted long. She sympathised, really, because
she had been very much the same as a child.

She had the pieces sewn up in a short time,
and when it looked something like a shirt,
though without the collar, she went out to
see if he had got over some of his ill-humour
and would like to try it on.

He wasn't in the back yard, and she came
inside again and glanced into his room, then
went out once more and called.

There was no answer. At first she wasn't
really worried, thinking he might be sulking
still, and hiding from her. But when after an
hour there was no sign of him, and she had
first unobtrusively searched and then, with
increasing shrillness in her voice, called and
called into the bush behind the house and up
and down the street, she began to panic.

The neighbours were mostly away during
the day, and the one or two who were home
couldn't help, they had seen nothing.

She searched the neighbourhood, debating whether she should ring Simon or the police, or both. Then she realised he would be home soon, anyway. When he did arrive, she was waiting for him on the drive, trying to keep her voice calm as she said, 'Simon, Benjy's missing.'

Simon rang the police, firing questions at Meredith and relaying to the anonymous voice on the phone how long the child had been missing, and what he was wearing. Meredith had a sudden thought. 'He might be trying to go to the farm, he wanted to visit your mother!'

He told them that and gave them directions, and when he had rung off said, 'I'll go and look in the car. You'll be all right here?'

He might come back. Someone had to stay here. She said, 'Yes. It was my fault, Simon, I'm sorry.'

She shivered at the look he threw her, tightlipped and unforgiving. 'Later,' he said briefly, and was out the door. She heard the car back out of the drive and take off quickly down the street.

She wondered if she should phone the farm, but if Benjy did turn up there, Mr and

Mrs Van Dyk would certainly contact her, and there was no point in worrying them unnecessarily. Better to wait and hope that he would be found soon.

The police brought Benjy back unharmed almost an hour later. He looked chastened when he entered with a large young constable behind him, but when Meredith opened her arms to him in overwhelming relief, he hugged her without reserve and began chattering about his ride in the police car until she interrupted the flow to fervently thank his escort.

'That's all right,' the constable grinned. Then, fixing Benjy with a stern eye, he added, 'But don't you go doing that again, my lad. You're too young to go visiting on your own, understand?'

Benjy nodded solemnly, and the constable ruffled the child's fair hair with a broad hand and took his leave.

She gave Benjy some mince on toast and was putting out fruit and custard for him when she heard Simon's car in the drive. Flying to the front door, she flung it open and cried as Simon slammed the car door behind him, 'He's here! He's all right.'

'I know,' he said, bounding grim-faced up the steps. 'The police told me they'd found him on the way to the farm.'

He walked past her straight into the kitchen where the light was on and Benjy sat at the table, a spoon in one hand. The child's eyes widened in trepidation as his father strode across, grasped his shoulders and lifted him off the chair, squatting down to his level as he set his feet on the floor. Simon's face was pale and very stern, his eyes blazing with emotion. 'Now, you listen to me,' he said, controlling his voice with obvious effort. 'Don't you *ever*, *ever*, do that again.' He shook the boy sharply, twice. 'You know you're not allowed off the section without a grown up. That was very, very naughty. Now tell Merrie you're sorry and you won't do it again.'

Benjy's eyes filled with tears, and his lips wobbled as he looked up at Meredith. 'I'm sorry, Merrie,' he gulped.

'It's all right,' Meredith said, going down beside him, her arm about his waist.

'*And you won't do it again!*' his father insisted.

Benjy scrubbed his eyes with a fist, sobbing.

'You're frightening him,' Meredith whispered to Simon.

He cast her a look that silenced her, and said quite gently to his son, 'Go on, Ben, say it.'

'W-won't do it again, Merrie,' Benjy blubbered and, as Simon removed his hands, turned into her waiting arms and wailed against her shoulder. She stood up, taking him with her, and Simon stood too, still looking white about the mouth, rigidly controlled.

'It was my fault,' she murmured, pausing to shush Benjy and kiss his temple, trying to comfort him. 'I snapped at him.'

Simon's brows contracted. 'For heaven's sake, Meredith, he can't take it into his head to run away from home every time you get a bit impatient! He shouldn't have done it, and he knows better, and he's lucky I didn't tan his hide for him!'

Simon had never lifted a finger to Benjy, she knew, and had from the first vetoed physical punishment except when the boy was very tiny and was running into danger. His anxiety and the relief from it were taking the form of anger, but she supposed he wasn't being unreasonable. Benjy knew perfectly well he had been naughty and disobedient, and she certainly didn't want any recurrence of the last few anxious hours. Perhaps it was as well to ram the lesson home.

Benjy's sobbing subsided quite quickly, and she sat him down with his pudding, ignoring Simon's sardonic glance at the plate of fruit and custard. He probably thought that she should have made Benjy go without, but she didn't see how that would help. 'Would you like some mince on toast?' she asked Simon. 'I'm afraid it's all there is.'

'What about you?' he asked. 'Have you eaten?'

'I don't want any,' she confessed. The tension had still not receded, and she wasn't hungry. 'I'll have something later.'

'I'll wait, too,' he said, and after standing for a few moments watching Benjy eat, he went into the other room.

She sent Benjy in to have his bath while she re-heated the mince, adding some herbs, mushroom stock and tomato juice to make it more interesting, and took out a carton of sour cream to stir in at the last minute.

She went to check on the truant and found

him struggling into pyjamas in his room. 'You put me to bed, Merrie,' he said, apparently still wary of his father's displeasure.

'All right,' she said, 'but I haven't time for a story because Daddy's had no tea yet. He was out looking for you and he missed it.'

Apparently Benjy realised the fairness of that, and in a few minutes she had kissed him and turned out the light.

In the living room she said to Simon, 'Aren't you going to say good night to him? He's in bed.'

'Already?' He looked up from the paper he was reading. 'That was quick.'

'I think he's trying to make up. Please go and see him. I'm sure he's really sorry.'

He got to his feet, and she went into the kitchen and put on some rice to boil. She still wasn't really hungry, but Simon ought to eat something. She got out the plates and sliced some French bread, putting the buttered pieces into a small basket. When Simon came in she said, 'How about lighting the fire, and we'll have this in the living room.' There was wood in a huge basket by the fireplace, and she felt they needed a nice relaxed atmosphere in which to unwind after the stress of the day.

'Okay,' he said. By the time she brought in the plates on a tray, the fire was crackling beautifully, and Simon had turned off the main light.

'Nice,' he said, tasting his meat. 'What is it?'

'I suppose a sort of poor man's stroganoff,' she said. 'It's more or less made up on the spur of the moment.'

'Well, it's all right,' he said.

He finished the plateful, and she ate all hers, too, surprisingly hungrier than she had realised. She took the plates out and made coffee, since neither of them wanted dessert, and carried it back to the fire.

They sat side by side on the rug, leaning against the sofa, and sipped their coffee slowly. The fire had lowered to a dim, comfortable glow, and when Simon put down his empty cup and reached over for more wood, she said, 'Don't. It's nice like that. I like it.'

He took her cup and placed it beside his, and curved his arms around her, so that her back rested against his chest, his face nuzzling her hair.

'You were a bit hard on poor Benjy,' she said.

'Serve the little brat right.'

'Simon! He's your son. And it *was* partly my fault. I shouldn't have snapped.'

'It wasn't your fault. He knows the rules. Having a tiff with you doesn't excuse him breaking them. Anyway, it's all over now. He went to sleep quite happily.'

'Oh, good.' She yawned, and he moved his head to smile down at her.

'The little beggar's tired you out. Meredith, don't think you've got to be the perfect mother, will you? All kids get snarled at occasionally by their parents, justifiably or otherwise. I have a feeling you've been trying to be a model of patience and forbearance. And you can't be. No one can. Least of all someone of your temperament.'

'Thanks!'

'You know what I mean. It just isn't natural for you not to show your feelings. Of course you won't lash out at him every time he annoys you, but you don't have to pretend that you're never annoyed. It won't damage him to know that parents have moods and offdays, too.'

'I have been feeling grumpy lately,' she admitted. 'Mostly because he has, since the measles. It's kind of rubbed off on me.'

'Mm, I've noticed,' he teased. There had been several nights lately when she had not felt like making love. Simon was good about it, but she felt a flush of compunction on her cheeks.

His hand moved over her shoulder, stroking, and she nestled closer to him and began toying with a button on his shirt, flipping it open and inserting her fingers in the gap. His lips played with her earlobe, and she undid another button and ran her hand over his skin, feeling with pleasure the rise and fall of his chest as he quickly drew breath.

He pushed her down on the rug and kissed her mouth and throat, and she linked her arms about his neck, opening her lips for him, arching her body into intimate contact with his.

He lifted his head and said, 'Would you rather go to bed while I do the dishes?'

Grimacing at him, she said, 'I'd rather go to bed with you. Blow the dishes!'

He laughed and kissed her again, and said

softly, 'What's wrong with here?'

'What if Benjy wakes up?' she whispered.

'Dead to the world,' he assured her, seeking her throat with his mouth, and she turned her head a little, allowing him better access. 'You know how he sleeps once he's off, and he's had an adventurous day.'

'How far did he go, actually? I forgot to ask.'

'About five miles, the policeman told me. Are you going to finish that job?'

'What job?'

'Undoing my shirt.'

'Do you want me to?'

He bit her ear gently. 'Do it, and I'll do the same for you.'

'An offer I can't refuse,' she admitted, laughing softly against his throat and sliding down to obey him, pressing light kisses on his skin as she deftly opened each button.

The fire burned lower, the black and grey of spent ashes encroaching on the red centre. But they didn't need it any more, wrapped in the engulfing heat of their mutual desire.

In the morning, Meredith awoke full of wellbeing, sitting up abruptly as she realised that Simon was no longer beside her.

He came in as she was reaching for the bedside clock, and she said, 'Have I slept in? What's the time?'

'I was just checking on the happy wanderer,' he said. 'It was so quiet I thought he might have decided to leave us again. You haven't slept in, but you might as well. He looks as though he's good for a few hours yet. Maybe we should take him on long walks more often. Knock out some of that surplus energy.'

'Your breakfast,' she said, making to push back the covers. He sat on the bed and firmly replaced them. He said, 'I got my own breakfast for years before you came on the scene, remember? You had a pretty hectic day too, yesterday. Have a lie-in, and stay there until the tyke wakes up and needs your eagle eye.'

He leaned over to give her a brief kiss, but his hands lingered on her shoulders, and he kissed her again, more deeply. 'You look so good in the mornings,' he said. 'Positively eatable.'

Meredith linked her hands behind his neck, smiling. 'The word is edible, actually.' She pulled him down to her and met his questing lips eagerly. Last night had been so good, she felt glowing with love.

He caressed her neck and shoulder as he kissed her, and his hand went to her breast and rested on it, his mouth moving erotically on hers.

When he raised his head, his hand stayed where it was, and he moved it experimentally, smiling into her eyes when he felt her inevitable arousal under his palm.

Meredith said huskily, 'How would you feel about skipping breakfast?'

His smile broadened, then he killed it and put on a considering face, while his fingers still caressed her, slipping inside her nightgown to make a more thorough exploration. 'It's a sacrifice,' he said. 'Do you think you can make it worth my while?'

'Beast!' She curled her fingers into a fist and aimed at his jaw, and he caught her wrist and fell, laughing, into her arms.

That day when she went to take her pill, she looked blankly at the extra one in the packet, and realised that she had totally forgotten to take it the night before.

It wouldn't matter, she told herself, going hot and cold as she stood with a glass of water in one hand and stared down at the telltale little disc, as though looking at it would make it disappear. It couldn't matter. Only, the instructions were quite specific. More than three hours later than usual was too late. Even last night there had probably been a chance of getting pregnant—certainly this morning. And for the next fourteen days, whether she took the rest of the course or not.

Simon came in, and with a guilty, reflexive action, she grabbed the packet and tried to hide it in her hand.

'The lamp in the living room's blown,' he explained, and opened a cupboard to take out a new light bulb.

As he closed the cupboard again he glanced at the corner of foil showing in her hand. 'Those pills don't disagree with you or anything, do they?'

Meredith shook her head. She must tell him. *Only I forgot to take one last night*. It was all she needed to say.

He said, 'Good,' and kissed her cheek as he went by, his eyes crinkling with faint amusement. 'It won't be forever,' he promised, and returned to the other room.

When she followed him a few moments later she said, 'Do you mean you'd be ready for a baby soon?'

He looked impatient. 'No. All I said was it won't be forever. Let's not get on to the subject again, Meredith. It isn't long since we talked it all out, and I find it wearing going over the same arguments every few weeks.'

Perhaps the choice is out of our hands, she thought. She had to tell him, but he was dropping the old bulb into the new packet and taking it through to the kitchen. He didn't look approachable.

It couldn't be very likely, she thought. One day without a pill. Probably nothing would happen. He was so against having a child just now, she dreaded his reaction. Why court his displeasure when there might be no need for it? Yesterday had been extraordinary, it wasn't likely to happen again.

He came back into the room and said, 'You're looking pensive. Something wrong?'

She shook her head. *Not yet. Maybe I'll never need to tell him.*

His arm came around her shoulders and he rubbed his chin against her temple. 'Tired?' he asked her.

'Yes.' She seized on the excuse. 'I think yesterday's catching up on me. I'll probably go to bed early.'

CHAPTER ELEVEN

IT was an excuse she was to use often in the next two weeks until the pills were supposed to be effective again. But she might as well not have bothered.

The morning that Benjy started school she felt horribly sick. It wasn't the first time, but it was the first time she had been unable to hide it from Simon. At breakfast he looked at her with a sharp frown and said, 'Are you off-colour? You look washed out.'

'I'm all right.' She managed a smile as she spread a minimum amount of butter on her toast. 'I think I'm more nervous than Ben about his first day at school.'

Simon's face relaxed. 'Goose! He's not so much nervous as excited. You'll have some time on your hands when he's away.'

'You know what I'd like to do with it,' she said, forcing the first mouthful of toast down. After the first, she knew, the rest would follow more easily, and when she had eaten the whole slice the awful nausea would subside a little.

Simon scraped back his chair and got up. 'Let's not start that again,' he said irritably. 'I'll go and wish the boy luck for his first day.'

She was going to the doctor this morning, as soon as she had settled Benjy in with his new teacher. He had already met her when the playcentre children who were shortly turning five visited the school, and she didn't forsee any problems. She had made the appointment with the doctor last week when she realised that it wasn't possible for any 'tummy bug' to follow the pattern that her nausea and other symptoms were following. Probably the birthday party she had put on for Benjy yesterday was responsible for her feeling worse than usual this morning. She hadn't eaten much, but just preparing the food had been enough to make her feel queasy, although she had liked doing it.

For days she had alternated between peaks of joyful hope and depths of nervous trepidation. She tried hard to maintain a calm outlook. If the doctor confirmed her own suspicions, Simon would just have to accept that their family was going to come along a little sooner than he had planned.

Benjy, with all the confidence in the world, waved her goodbye and turned to his teacher, and when she picked him up after school he was still bubbling with enthusiasm. She listened as well as she could to his excited description of his day, but when he had relayed it all over again to Simon that evening and finally been tucked into bed, she breathed a sigh of relief.

She was sitting on the sofa staring into the fire when Simon came in with two glasses of white wine. She took one, sipped at it and then set it down carefully on the end table as he sat beside her.

'No?' he said, indicating her glass.

She shook her head. 'You finish yours.'

He slipped an arm about her and finished the drink at leisure while she waited, growing more and more tense. When at last he put his glass down and made to draw her closer, she said quickly, 'Simon, I went to the doctor today——'

'You *were* sick this morning!' he said. 'Why didn't you say so? I would have taken Ben——'

'No, listen,' she said urgently, putting a hand on his arm. 'I'm not sick really. I'm—

pregnant.'

There was a long, long, silence. Then his hands gripped her shoulders and he held her away from him, his accusing gaze boring into her face. Harshly he said, *'What?'*

'Pregnant,' she repeated, daring to raise her eyes to his. Her heart dipped in fear because he looked terribly angry. His face was white, his mouth had thinned alarmingly, and his eyes were filled with an icy rage.

'How?' he demanded, his hands tightening on her shoulders until they hurt.

'I—I missed a pill,' she faltered. 'Just one.'

'One's enough, isn't it?' he said, and suddenly let her go, standing up to loom over her. *'You stubborn, self-willed, little wretch!* You wanted a baby, so you decided to start playing Russian roulette with your pills. I might have known you couldn't be trusted——'

'Simon!'

He ignored her. 'You're so bloody pig-headed, Meredith. I thought you'd grown up at last, but you've no more sense than when you were eight years old, and you're just as determined to get your own way, come hell or high water. You managed to plan it beautifully, didn't you? Just when Benjamin starts school——'

'I didn't plan it!' she protested.

'Don't tell me,' he said with angry sarcasm. 'It just happened, just when *you* wanted it, but quite by accident! What an idiot I was, thinking you'd never go behind my back!'

'I *didn't*!' she cried, distressed. 'It was an accident, Simon, I just forgot!'

'Forgot!' he said scornfully.

'The night Benjy went missing!' she said. 'Surely you can understand? I was so worried!'

'He was home long before the time you had to take it!'

'Well, yes, but then everything was late, and we had tea here in the lounge, and— well, you know what happened afterwards.'

He looked, if anything, more furious than ever, his eyes narrowed and glittering, his voice icy. 'Are you blaming *me*?'

'No. I'm not blaming anyone. I mean, I know I should have remembered, but I didn't, and we're having a baby.' Her eyes stung with tears. 'Simon, I know you think it's too soon, but it's happened. Please—can't we just be glad?'

'No,' he said coldly. 'I'm not glad. I feel sick to my stomach. I don't want this baby. *I don't want it!* '

She stood up, putting out her hands to touch him, draw him close to her. 'You can't mean that!' she said. 'Not really, it isn't true!'

'It is true and I mean it,' he said, flinging her hands away with a violent sweep of his arm. 'Don't touch me, Meredith,' he added between his teeth. 'I could *hit* you for what you've done. Just leave me alone, will you? I'm going out.'

She watched in horror as he flung out of the room, and heard with stunned disbelief the slam of the front door as he left.

He came back very late, and she had been lying in bed listening for him for hours. If he had glanced at her he would have seen that she was awake, but he didn't, even when he got into bed beside her; and after a while his regular breathing told her that he was asleep.

She was heavy-eyed and wan in the morning, and he said, 'You'd better go back to bed. I'll phone the refinery and tell them I'll be late, and then take Ben to school.'

'No,' she said.

'You're not fit——' he started angrily.

'I'll do it!' she told him with undue fierceness, determined not to give in. She wanted to show him that being pregnant wasn't going to make one iota of difference to her caring for Benjy. It was a matter of pride, now, of principle.

'Meredith——'

'I said I'll do it!' she reiterated. 'I'm all right.' Then she fled to the bathroom.

When she came out, he was hovering outside. She looked at him defiantly and said quite truthfully, 'I'm better now. You can go.'

His mouth tightened, and he left without kissing her goodbye. For the rest of the week they existed in a state of armed truce, mouthing polite nothings at each other, sleeping apart in the same bed, putting on a front of false cheerfulness for Benjy's sake whenever he was around.

At the weekend they went to the Van Dyks'. Simon made no suggestion of telling his family about the baby, and Meredith didn't dare to broach the subject. Anneke was home for the weekend, and after lunch Meredith asked her friend to walk with her over to her parents' home.

As they walked down the drive where rows of daffodils and jonquils were just coming into bloom under the red-leaved photinias, Meredith said abruptly, 'Anneke—what exactly caused Jill's death?'

Anneke cast her a slightly surprised look. 'It was a cerebral haemorrhage—she must have had an aneurism—a weak spot in an artery of the brain. There'd be no symptoms, but the strain of labour caused it to burst.'

'Simon was quite happy about Benjy, wasn't he? I mean, about Jill being pregnant?'

'Happy? He was over the moon. They both were. I'd have thought you'd remember. They'd been trying for a couple of years and she'd already miscarried once.'

'I didn't know that!' Meredith's head whipped round as she stared.

'Well, it's the sort of thing that gets kept in the family. But you're family, now.' Anneke looked at her sideways and said slowly, 'I suppose it's not something you can very easily talk to Simon about. It must be awkward, having a husband who's been married before. You'd feel as if you were prying if you asked him about his relationship with Jill.'

'Yes,' Meredith admitted in a low voice. 'But there are things I need to know, Anneke. You do understand, don't you?'

'Yes, I think so. And I don't suppose Simon would mind, really.' They walked on in silence for a while, and then Anneke said, 'After she died he felt guilty about having kept on trying. He said he should have realised that the miscarriage was a warning and made her give up.'

'Oh, but surely——'

'Of course he couldn't have known. No one could. The incidence of miscarriage in first pregnancies is very high. People always think of things they could have done, or shouldn't have done, when a person dies. It's part of the grieving process. But he got over that in time. It was just a horrible accident and there was no way he could have prevented it, any more than if she'd been run over by a car. Of course, having Benjy to think of must have helped. And now he has you. It's nice to see him really happy again instead of just coping with life.'

Meredith smiled automatically and walked on. She had hoped for some enlightenment but had found none. Nothing made any sense.

On Monday at the hairdresser's she picked up a magazine and read an article about 'Your First Baby'. One of the common problems, the writer said, was the father's jealousy of the new baby. The wife must be on her guard, and not devote all her attention to the baby at the expense of her husband.

Was that all it was? Meredith wondered. Simon had said more than once that he wanted her to himself for a while. And yet she couldn't believe that he was so immature. It might have been possible in his first marriage, when he had been younger and didn't already have a child. It hardly seemed likely in the present circumstances.

Still, she was clutching at straws now. Anything was worth trying. Perhaps he did resent her preoccupation with the question of a baby. Maybe he really felt that she saw him more as a means to an end than a person she loved in his own right. He had accused her of it once. Possibly he had even meant it.

She gave Benjy an early meal that evening, a hot dog and chips so that he would feel it was a special treat, and when Simon arrived she said, 'Dinner will be late for you and me, after Benjy's in bed. Would you like a snack now and a cup of tea?'

He shook his head, looking slightly bemused, and she said, 'Could you see Benjy into bed, then? I'm rather busy in the kitchen.'

He came back in as she was stirring a sauce and watching anxiously for lumps.

'Is this a special occasion?' he asked rather dryly. He must have seen the low table she had drawn up in front of the sofa, covered with a pretty cloth and holding two candlesticks with red candles in them.

'Sort of,' she said evasively. 'I'm making it one, anyway. I bought some wine. Can you pour it, please?'

He said, 'Do you want to start now?' and handed her a glass.

She sipped with one hand while stirring with the other, then put down the glass to remove the pot and turn off the heat. 'It's ready now, anyway.'

'We're eating in the other room, I presume?' he asked.

'Yes. Take the wine in, and I'll bring the food.'

She dished up, whipped off her apron to reveal one of her prettiest dresses, fingered her hair, and took the plates in. Simon had lit the candles, and was lounging in a corner of the sofa, his glass in his hand, his eyes on the fire she had started earlier, although the weather wasn't particularly cold.

She had made a casserole dish, so that it was easy to eat with just a fork and they could comfortably sit on the sofa with their plates held one-handed.

'How was work?' she asked, and his eyes crinkled with slightly cynical amusement, but at least he smiled, if a little tightly.

'As usual,' he said. 'I know the little woman is supposed to enquire into her man's day, but I don't really want to talk about work.'

She looked down at her plate, digging her fork into a cube of meat. 'Well, what would you like to talk about?'

'That's a question guaranteed to make anyone dry up. Isn't this the kind of meal that should be accompanied by soft music?'

'Oh, I forgot!' She uncurled her legs and made to put her plate down on the table.

'I'll do it.' He forestalled her, going over to the radiogram in the corner and putting on a recording of slow, dreamy orchestral music.

'All right?' he asked her as he returned to his seat.

'Perfect.' She glanced at him as he picked up his dinner again, wondering if she had imagined the slight edge to his voice.

The music filled the silence as they ate, and when the plates were empty she took them to the kitchen and brought back the cold fruit and mousse dessert with hot chocolate sauce that had taken ages to prepare.

'You've got to admire it before you eat it,' she said, placing the two glass dishes on the table.

He smiled, and her heart lightened. It was the first genuine smile he had given her in days.

'Very impressive,' he said. 'But does it taste as good as it looks?'

'I don't know. I've never made it before.'

'What's this all in aid of?' he asked.

'I think you know.' She suddenly met his eyes squarely. 'I didn't do it on purpose, Simon. I swear to you I didn't. Oh, perhaps my subconscious had something to do with it. But I wouldn't have ever cheated on you like that deliberately. Surely you know——'

Her voice trembled and stopped, and a

tear slid hotly down her cheek.

Simon reached out his hand and pulled her head down to his shoulder. 'No, you wouldn't,' he said slowly, his hand stroking her hair. 'I know.'

'Oh, Simon,' she sighed, her hand clutching at his shirt front. 'I'm sorry. I love you.'

He raised her head with his hand under her chin and kissed her. 'I'm sorry, too. I spoiled your big news, didn't I?'

'It doesn't matter. I knew you wouldn't be pleased, really, because it was too soon. Only I didn't realise you'd be quite so angry. I thought you'd get over it, and be glad. It's *our* child, not just mine. And I wouldn't want it if I didn't love you so much.'

He looked down at her with something that might have been a hint of scepticism. 'What about Michael?' he asked.

'Michael?' she said scornfully. 'Puppy love. I haven't thought of him in months. Surely you know that!'

'I suspected it.'

'I love *you*, Simon,' she said earnestly, determined to convince him of it. 'Even if you couldn't give me a baby I'd still love you, but you have, and—if it's possible, it's made me love you even more.'

His smile was wry. 'Yes, I have. And I suppose I'll just have to accept it.'

Uncertainly, she said, 'Why is it so hard? You didn't really mean it when you said you don't want it, did you?'

'What's done is done,' he said, loosening his hold on her. 'That concoction is melting. Is it supposed to?'

'No, you're supposed to eat it before it gets a chance to,' she said, reaching for the dishes, glancing at him doubtfully as she handed him one. Stoic acceptance was less than she had hoped for, but perhaps it was all she could expect. She felt a little spurt of exasperated anger. He had made a decision to wait, against her wishes, and not only she, but nature itself, was to abide by that, apparently. Maybe he had become a little too accustomed to making decisions for others, and perhaps she had let him go on treating her like a younger sister for too long. He didn't necessarily know best just because he was older. 'You can't always order life exactly to your specifications,' she reminded him. 'Sometimes things just don't go according to plan.'

'Do you think *I* don't know that?' he asked violently, and she remembered Jill and cringed.

Shaking her head, she muttered, 'I'm sorry. I guess I'm just disappointed that you're not happier about the baby.'

'Give me time,' he said rather wearily. 'You always tend to expect too much, Meredith. Try to ease up a little, hmm?'

When he put down his empty dish, she said, 'Was it okay?'

'Yes. It lived up to its appearance. I'll make the coffee, shall I?'

She nodded, happy enough to stay where she was. She smiled at him a little anxiously when he came back with the cups, and afterwards they sat companionably side by side, his arm about her shoulders, her hair against his cheek. When he began kissing her, she responded eagerly, and some minutes later she murmured, 'Let's go to bed.'

It was just as good as ever, his caresses driving her frantic with desire until she was hovering on the edge, waiting for him to take her over the brink, but he seemed to be hesitating, holding back. Frustrated and puzzled, she suddenly realised that something was badly wrong. Unable to believe what was happening, she pulled his head down to hers and kissed him with desperate passion, and he reciprocated, his hands biting into her shoulders, his mouth bruising. But then he suddenly broke away from her and rolled over on his back, his hand over his eyes. 'It's no good,' he said harshly. 'I can't.'

Stunned, she raised herself on one elbow to stare at his dark shape beside her. 'Simon——' she said tentatively, stretching out a hand, only to have it knocked away from him. 'What's the matter?'

'Can't you *tell* what's the matter?' he asked.

'I mean—why?'

'Oh, shut up, Meredith. I don't *know* why! It never happened with——'

With Jill. The name he hadn't spoken echoed clearly in her mind.

'What about—anyone else?' she asked, almost whispering.

For a few moments he didn't answer. Then he said heavily, 'There's never been anyone else, Meredith. Only Jill—and you.'

Abruptly she lay back on her own pillow. She felt a mixture of gladness and fright. His hand touched her arm.

'I'm—sorry,' he said. 'Can I do something for you, darling?'

'No!' she said sharply. 'I'm all right.'

She felt humiliated as well as shocked. He hadn't really wanted to make love to her, only she had set the scene so carefully and it must have been obvious that she had in mind a passionate reconciliation. She had practically seduced him, and he had gone along with it until his body rejected her of its own accord. Women could pretend passion—not that she had ever needed to with him—but men could only fake it up to a certain point. She turned her back on him, curled herself into a ball under the blankets, and waited for sleep to come.

CHAPTER TWELVE

IT wouldn't happen again, she told herself, though she was careful to let him make the overtures next time. And it did happen again. Appalled, she realised that he too was shaken by the incident, but when she tried clumsily to tell him it didn't matter he brushed her off with impatience. He didn't want to talk about it, and after the same thing happened a third time, he stopped trying.

She lived in a vacuum, going through the motions of daily life, studying for her next playcentre certificate, caring for Benjy and taking him to see his grandparents, though less often now, cooking and cleaning as usual, even joking with Simon and kissing him as he left for work and when he came home. But in bed every night he turned on his side and went to sleep without touching her.

She knew that she ought to be reassuring him with sympathy and understanding, boosting his self-confidence. But she didn't know how to begin. Simon had always been the one who did the comforting, the encouraging, the protecting. She tried, but her tentative efforts brought a chilly reaction that froze her out, and after a while she discovered in herself an inescapable resentment.

She was sure there was nothing physically wrong with Simon. He might have been tired, once, or there could have been some other physiological reason. But not three times. She believed that some men found pregnancy unattractive, but she hadn't even begun to show signs of it yet, excepting a slight extra fullness in her breasts and an indiscernible alteration in her waist measurement.

It must be her pregnancy that had caused the problem. He was still angry with her, hadn't really forgiven her for what he saw as her fault. And yet it was unlike Simon to carry a grudge like that.

She recalled that Anneke had said he felt guilty after Jill's death, for continuing to try and start a family. Perhaps he hadn't got over it, as Anneke had thought. Could his buried guilt feelings have surfaced now, knowing Meredith was carrying his child?

But when she ventured to suggest something of the sort, he stared at her as though she had gone quite crazy, and said crushingly, 'Let's cut out the amateur psychology, Meredith. Jill died because she had a pre-existing condition that no one could have suspected. It was nobody's fault. Certainly not mine.'

He seemed terribly well adjusted to it, and she had to admit that her tentative conclusion must have been wrong. But there was no denying that his attitude now was in a stark, unmistakable contrast to the way he and Jill had planned and longed for a child. The other possible reason that kept rising insidiously to mind she tried to discount, unable to bear the implications. But the suspicion kept nibbling at the edges of her consciousness, growing stronger as she and Simon seemed to be drifting further and further apart. He had wanted Jill's baby, but not Meredith's. He had made a child with Jill out of their love for each other. He hadn't felt ready to make one with Meredith because he didn't love her enough to welcome it. He had tried, and until she became pregnant he had been able to fool her, perhaps even himself. As long as he thought there was no chance of conceiving a baby, there was no problem. But now his body would no longer obey him.

Perhaps deep down he felt he was being unfaithful to Jill's memory. He had loved her with a deep and abiding passion. Whatever fondness he had for Meredith, it wasn't strong enough for him to want a child by her. His mind rejected the child, and his body reciprocated by rejecting its mother.

She told herself she shouldn't be hurt, and certainly it should be no surprise. Simon had made no great protestations of undying passion to her. She had known when he suggested marriage that what he felt was little more than fondness, and if she had tumbled head over heels in love very soon afterwards she could hardly expect him to have done the same. And yet—they had been so happy. She *knew* he had been happy.

But she was second best, and that was hard to accept. Simon was right, she did expect too much. Second best wasn't good enough for her, and the thought brought a hard knot of angry grief to her throat. But there wasn't a thing she could do about it.

When she found she couldn't get into her jeans any more, she said to Simon, 'We'll have to tell our parents about the baby.'

He said, 'I assumed you'd have told yours.'

She shook her head. Her mother had been giving her some questioning looks lately, but Simon, although he was being extra helpful and careful of her, seemed to want to ignore the fact of the coming baby altogether. He never mentioned it. She felt he wanted to deny its existence, and once their respective families knew about it, that certainly would become impossible.

'Well, we'll be seeing them this weekend, won't we?' he said. 'You can tell them then.'

She had pictured Simon holding her hand while they did so together. Determinedly she put the picture out of her mind.

'You've been feeling better lately, haven't you?' he asked her suddenly.

'Yes.' The morning sickness had almost gone, and she had begun to feel less lethargic. Physically she was full of wellbeing, in spite of the constant ache that seemed to have settled around her heart, and the strain of lying in bed each night longing to reach out a hand and touch him, but not daring to.

She was anxious about the way he would receive the inevitable congratulations, but she needn't have worried. A little bitterly, she reflected that he should have been an actor. His imitation of a proud father-to-be and loving husband couldn't have been faulted. For some reason it angered her, and she was still nursing a simmering resentment when they got home. Nor did it subside after they had eaten and Benjy had gone to bed. When Simon came back from saying good night to his son, she was prowling round the lounge, rearranging cushions and picking up the odd toy that Benjy had left lying around.

'Why don't you leave that?' he said, watching her fish a small plastic car from under the sofa. 'Aren't you tired?'

'Someone has to do it,' she snapped. 'And I'll probably still be tired tomorrow.'

He looked at her sharply. 'Are you resting enough? Has the doctor given you some iron pills?'

'Yes, I am, and yes, he did, and what do you care, anyway?'

'Don't be ridiculous!' He came into the room, scowling. 'Of course I care!'

'Oh, about your childminder-housekeeper, perhaps,' she said sarcastically. 'But you don't give a fig for me as a person, as your wife!'

He went white, his mouth thinning

ominously. 'That's unfair.'

'Yes,' she said, flinging back her head. 'I suppose it is. It's all I have any right to expect, really, isn't it?'

'Oh, what the hell are you talking about?' he said, shaking his head irritably. 'I'm sorry, I don't feel like indulging your obvious desire for a good row at the moment.'

'That remark's typical of you!' she flashed.

'In what way?' he enquired coldly.

'Patronising! Patronising and oh, so superior. And I'm sick of it!'

'Of what, precisely?' He stood with his hands in his pockets, looking controlled and cool, inflaming her temper still further.

'Of your whole attitude! You're like some little tin god, laying down the law and making all the decisions, and I'm supposed to obey without question——'

'Hah!' he interrupted. 'I'd like to see the day!'

But she wasn't to be stopped now. '—like a good little child-wife. Well, I'm not a child any more, I'm not your little sister's friend that you can boss and order about, play the Dutch uncle with. I'm a grown woman, whether you like it or not. I'm your wife, and

I'm having your baby. I know you don't like the idea, but you'll just have to live with it. I'm sorry, but if you didn't want any children that are not Jill's, you shouldn't have married me—or anyone!'

His hands left his pockets, and he said, 'You don't know what you're talking about!' But she had rushed past him, trying to avert the threat of tears, not wanting him to see. She thrust open the door of Benjy's room and dropped the toys into the basket at the foot of his bed, straightening to see him move, his eyes open in the darkness.

'Merrie?' he said.

'I'm sorry, darling,' she said unsteadily. 'Did I wake you up?'

'I wasn't asleep. What are you and Daddy doing?'

'Just talking,' she said.

'You talk loud.'

In spite of herself, she had to smile. 'We didn't mean to disturb you.'

'What's disturb?'

'Keep you awake,' she explained. 'Anyway, go to sleep now, there's a good boy.' She went over to kiss him, and he said, 'Are we going to have a baby sister?'

'A sister or brother,' she said. 'But we have to wait a while yet.' They had meant to leave it a bit longer before telling him, but perhaps he had picked up some of the conversation among the adults today . . .

'Till Christmas?'

'Longer than that. Quite a long time. Come on, snuggle down. We can talk about it tomorrow.'

She closed the door softly as she left the room. The angry tears had receded, leaving her dry-eyed but drained.

Simon was in their room when she entered it, standing at the window with his hands on his hips, staring out into the dark. He turned as she came in and said, 'What did you mean by that last crack, exactly?'

'Nothing,' she said tiredly, her mouth drooping. 'Let's not argue any more, Simon. You said you didn't want to.'

He looked at her broodingly until she dropped her eyes, and went to the bed and lifted the pillow to get her nightdress. Then he turned and tugged the curtains closed.

She woke suddenly, dragged from sleep by some sound that set her heart pounding, her eyes wide and dazed, searching the darkness without knowing why.

Then it came again, a deep, masculine moan of anguish, and Simon stirred restlessly beside her, his slurred voice saying, 'No. My darling, *no*. Don't die! *Please don't die.*'

She turned to him quickly, leaning over him as his head moved jerkily from side to side on the pillow. 'Simon!'

He moaned again, and even in the darkness she could see the faint sheen of sweat on his forehead. 'No,' he said again, and then, with a sound like a choking sob, 'NO!'

'Simon!' She shook his shoulder. 'Simon, it's a dream! It's all right. Wake up.'

He shuddered, and his breath seemed to stop. Then his eyes flickered briefly open and he put up his hand to feel hers on his shoulders, then slid his fingers up her arm. 'Oh, God,' he said, on a note of deep relief. 'A dream. You're not dead—oh, my darling, I couldn't bear it!' His arms came round her and pulled her down to him, and his cheek felt burning hot and damp with sweat. His hand feverishly stroked her hair. 'Not dead,' he whispered, and was instantly asleep again.

She lay against him, held in his sleeping

embrace, and tears trickled from her closed lids. He had been dreaming of Jill's death and thought it was Jill comforting him, telling him it wasn't true. He had gone to sleep again thinking it was her in his arms.

Meredith's heart contracted with pain for him. It wasn't his fault that he had loved Jill more and still grieved for her in his dreams. Perhaps he was dreaming of Jill now, of the happiness that they had shared.

Hopelessly, she wondered if the memories would ever fade, if she could ever begin to replace his dead love. She had to try, it was the only way to make their marriage work.

In the morning she woke first, and started to ease herself away from him, but the movement must have disturbed him. His slack arms tightened about her shoulders, and he opened his eyes. As she lifted her head and looked into them, she saw a strange expression in the blue depths, before he said huskily, on a note of enquiry, 'Hello?'

Feeling a need to explain, she said almost defensively, 'You had a dream—a nightmare.'

'I remember,' he said. 'God, it was

horrible.' His hand on her shoulder gripped suddenly, bruisingly, and she said foolishly, 'It's all right now.' Of course it wasn't all right, Jill was dead, and he probably wished he hadn't woken this morning and discovered that his nightmare was true. She wondered how many other mornings he had woken to the same cruel realisation.

She stirred again, and he said, 'Don't go away, not yet.' He closed his eyes, pushing her head down again on to his shoulder, and she supposed, with a faint sensation of gladness, that if she wasn't Jill she was at least someone to hold on to for comfort. At the moment, with the memory of his distress last night still fresh, she didn't mind. It was enough that he wanted her here, close to him, that she could give him her silent sympathy and compassion, and that he seemed to need it.

They had slept late. Benjy had been invited to a birthday party, and he got up and made himself breakfast and virtuously tidied his room before he crept into theirs. Seeing Meredith awake, as she turned her head and moved slightly away from Simon, he touched her face with a slightly sticky hand, saying,

'Merrie? Will you take me to the birthday?'

'What time is it?' She peered at the bedroom clock and said, 'It's all right, Benjy. Mrs Robinson said eleven o'clock. There's a whole hour to go yet.' She must get up, she thought reluctantly. She pulled back the covers and went to the window to open the curtains. Simon blinked and groaned dramatically.

Benjy climbed up on the bed and sat on his father's feet, demanding a ride, and Meredith laughed as she put on a dressing gown, watching Simon's pretence of sleep in the face of his son's determined efforts to wake him.

She took Benjy to the party and stayed a little while to help Tim's mother prepare the table, then returned home to find Simon making toast and heating soup in the kitchen. 'Want some?' he asked her. 'Or have you filled up with disgusting goodies from the party?'

'Heavens, no. They haven't even started yet. I shouldn't think Benjy will want any tea, though. They've got a real spread there.'

'Can't be better than what you put on for Ben's birthday.'

'Aw, gee, that was nothing,' she said mock-modestly.

Simon grinned. 'I was sorry for you, putting so much time into making the cake and all those other things look so terrific, only to have the little monsters demolish the lot in about ten minutes flat.'

'It wasn't that much trouble, really, I took a lot of short cuts. Anyway, I enjoyed it.'

'You like being a mother, don't you?' he asked, putting two bowls of soup on the table.

'I think I was cut out for it,' she said as she sat down.

He joined her and passed her a piece of toast. 'You're certainly looking blooming on it,' he observed. 'Feeling all right?'

He never referred to her pregnancy, even obliquely, unless it was to express some concern for her health.

'I feel wonderful,' she told him. 'You don't need to worry about me.' She tried the soup. It was on the tip of her tongue to ask if he remembered last night and his nightmare, but before she spoke he said, 'When do we pick up Ben? Do you want to go out somewhere this afternoon?'

'Five o'clock,' she said, laughing as he raised his brows and murmured, 'Tim's mother must be a tiger for punishment.'

'And I don't think I want to go out,' she added. It would be nice for the two of them to be alone. Not long ago she would have predicted with accuracy exactly what they would do with an afternoon to themselves, but things were different now.

Anneke phoned just after lunch. She had not been home on Saturday, though an excited Mrs Van Dyk had telephoned her with news of the coming baby. 'She'd like to come round,' Meredith told Simon. 'She's bringing someone to meet us. I invited them for tea.'

'Oh?' he said. 'We haven't seen her much lately. Is the someone she's bringing the reason, do you think?'

'Quite likely. His name's Patrick and he's a doctor. I think maybe she's bringing him here as a sort of trial run before taking him to meet your family.'

'Well, I shall look him over and demand to know his intentions and his prospects, then.'

'You dare!' she said, laughing. 'Anneke

would never speak to you again!'

It turned out to be a pleasant afternoon and evening. Benjy was delighted to find his aunt there when Simon brought him home, and even Patrick managed to show a flattering interest in his description of the party. They opened a bottle of wine with dinner. Anneke had two glasses, but Meredith, being careful, stopped at one. When they had eaten, and Benjy had been read to and tucked up by Anneke, Simon began pouring whisky for himself and Patrick, who was entertaining company and almost as talkative as Anneke. It was after midnight when they left, and Simon yawned as they heard the engine note of the car fade down the street. 'Coming to bed?' he asked as Meredith picked up the glasses to carry them to the kitchen.

'Yes, of course.' Once he would have come over and put his arms about her, perhaps repeated the question with an added meaning, but tonight he stood in the doorway for a moment watching her, and then turned away.

It would get better, she assured herself. She would have to learn to settle for what Simon could give her and not demand more than he had ever promised. Maybe that was the root cause of the problem. She had let him know how much she loved him and made him feel guilty about being unable to return it. He had asked her once to ease off. Perhaps if she played it cool, made it less obvious how she felt, he wouldn't feel so pressured and things would come right. They had been easier with each other today, more natural. The terrifying rift was healing, although a dark shadow still lay over their happiness.

When she joined him in the bedroom, she was surprised to see that he had a glass of whisky on the dressing table. He was pulling off his shirt, pausing to take a sip before unbuckling his belt.

She got undressed and used the bathroom, and when she came back he was sitting on the bed in his pyjama trousers, finishing the drink.

He looked up and went into the bathroom without a word, and when he came back he turned off the light and got into the bed beside her and sighed heavily.

He reached out an arm and put it round her, pulling her over to lie against him, her shoulders resting against his chest. 'I've drunk too much,' he confessed, rubbing his chin over her hair. 'Sorry, my love.'

She dared to tease. 'Dutch courage?'

After a moment he laughed a little. 'No. It isn't that.'

'You have drunk a lot tonight,' she ventured. 'What's the matter?'

He sighed again, and his arm tightened slightly about her. 'Silly, really. It's that damned dream. It's been haunting me all day. Can't get it out of my head.'

'It's not silly,' she said, twisting to face him. 'Try to forget it, Simon.' She kissed him softly, tentatively—hoping, but afraid to be too aggressive in case it wasn't what he wanted.

He lifted his hands to hold her head, and took over the kiss, turning to push her back against the pillows, touching her face and neck and then her breast. Then he buried his lips in her neck. 'No,' he said. 'Not when I'm half tipsy. It wouldn't be fair to you, and drink is notoriously apt to impair a man's performance. Darling, do you mind if I just hold you until I go to sleep?'

'Of course I don't mind.' She stroked his hair, filled with a melting tenderness. He sounded almost pleading, something new in her experience, as though he needed her there to keep away the dark dream. 'It's all right,' she murmured, her arm cradling him. 'Go to sleep.'

But the whisky and her arms couldn't keep the dream from returning. He had slipped from her hold and turned away as he slept, and she woke to hear him gasping in distress. She touched his cheek and her fingertips came away wet, and she knew he was crying in his sleep.

When she woke him, he grasped at her as if he was drowning, and choked out, 'I won't *let* you! *I won't let it happen.*'

'Simon,' she said urgently. 'Wake up! It's *Meredith*!'

He gave a great shuddering sigh, and said, 'Meredith. Hold me, please, darling. Let me hold you.'

She went into his arms and wound hers tightly about him. 'You were dreaming about Jill again,' she said. 'It's only a dream, Simon. That's all over now.'

'Jill?' he said slowly, his speech slurred. 'It isn't Jill I dream about. It's you.'

'Me?' She raised her head, trying to see his face in the darkness.

'Hold me,' he muttered. His hand came up behind her head, pulling her down to him again. 'I was so frightened. There was nothing I could do but watch it happen all over again.'

'What?' she asked softly, fumbling for his hand and holding it tightly.

'You——' he groaned, '—dying.'

She went cold. 'That was Jill,' she said, bringing his hand to her cheek. 'I'm not dying, Simon. I'm perfectly all right.'

He moved his head restlessly. 'You're having my baby.'

'Simon!' she breathed. His speech was slurred, but she understood exactly what he was saying. She struggled out of his arms to switch on the lamp, and leaned over him as he blinked in the sudden glare. She grasped his shoulders and said, 'Simon, listen! What happened to Jill was an *accident*, a terrible, freakish accident. It won't happen to me, it can't! I'm perfectly healthy. *I'm not going to die!*'

His face was pale, and his eyes looked glazed. Gradually they cleared, and he passed a hand over his forehead. 'No, of course not,' he muttered. 'I'm sorry, I'm not making sense, am I? It was that dream again.'

'Yes,' she said, looking at him anxiously. 'I know.'

'Turn the light off,' he asked her drowsily, closing his eyes. 'I'm all right, now.'

'You're sure? Can I get you something?'

He shook his head slightly. 'Stay with me,' he muttered. 'Don't go away.'

She switched off the light and lay down with her head on his shoulder, his arm curved about her. 'Sorry, love,' he said indistinctly. 'Guess I had too much whisky.' He muttered something else she couldn't catch, about 'nightmares'.

She felt his chest rise in a sigh, and then his breathing slowed and evened out and she knew he was asleep again.

She lay awake for a time, her brain trying to bring order to random thoughts and memories. If she could only concentrate, she thought, irritably. But she was tired, her head muzzy from the sudden awakening, and after a while she too drifted into sleep.

CHAPTER THIRTEEN

ON Monday she went shopping after lunch and bought some fine primrose wool, knitting needles, and a pattern for a baby's jacket. She hadn't knitted for years, but as a child she had learned, and for a while had spent a lot of her time making knitted clothes for her dolls. So far she had nothing for the baby, and now that it was an open secret it was time some preparations were made.

At the library she found the shelf on child-care, and borrowed several books on pregnancy, birth and early childhood, and then she decided that she would pick up Benjy from school. Usually he walked home with a couple of little friends who had an older sister to keep an eye on them, but today she waited outside the school for him and took him off with her for a special afternoon tea in a coffee bar.

Back home, she dumped the books and small parcels on the table and they sat down on the sofa together for Benjy to do his reading-aloud homework for her.

'Very good,' she said when he had finished, and stood up. A strange fluttering in her stomach made her put her hand to it with a surprised little exclamation, and Benjy said, 'Have you got a tummy ache, Merrie?'

She looked down at him and laughed, her face flushing with excitement. 'No, not a tummy ache. I think it's the baby kicking.' Once or twice before she had thought she felt it, but this was definite, a series of positive little movements, too strong to be anything else.

'Is baby kicking you?' Benjy asked, his eyes wide with surprise. 'Does it hurt?'

'No,' she assured him, sitting down beside him on the sofa and putting her arm about his shoulder. 'It's too little to hurt me. It just sort of tickles.'

Benjy chuckled and put his hand where she had placed hers. 'Will it tickle me?'

When Simon came home Benjy met him at the door, dragging him into the kitchen to see Meredith. 'Baby kicks!' he announced. 'You feel, Daddy—she tickles.'

Meredith saw the shuttered look come down on Simon's face before he smiled at

Benjy and then, enquiringly, at her.

'Feel, Daddy,' Benjy insisted, as Simon put an arm about Meredith and kissed her briefly.

Meredith said, 'I think baby's gone to sleep now, Benjy.'

'Oh. Then don't disturb her, Daddy,' Benjy said, making his father's brows rise in amusement.

'Are you all right?' he asked her when Benjy had gone off to find his latest drawing to show his father.

'Great. I hadn't felt the baby move before—not positively. Benjy's about as excited as I am.'

There was something strained about his smile. 'Yes. It's quite a thrill, isn't it?'

Perhaps, having been through it before, he just wasn't able to summon the enthusiasm of a first-time parent. Or perhaps he couldn't help remembering Jill going through the same exciting time, and the tragic outcome. Thoughtfully, she turned to mix a sauce as Benjy came back with his picture.

After they had eaten, Simon put Benjy to bed while Meredith washed up and put the kettle on. They had developed a habit of having coffee in the lounge after Benjy's bedtime. When Simon returned to the kitchen she silently handed him his cup and followed with her own as he went into the next room. Simon switched on the television for the news, and although she cast him one or two surreptitious glances, he seemed to be absorbed in the programme.

She finished her coffee and waited for his cup, then took them both into the kitchen and rinsed them out. The packet containing the wool, needles and pattern she had bought was on the bench, and after a few moments she slowly unwrapped it and took the things into the lounge.

She sat on the sofa opposite his easy chair and began casting on stitches. She had knitted two rows before Simon looked up and stared a little. Meredith dropped a stitch and, keeping her eyes firmly down, carefully picked it up. After a moment, his voice neutral, he asked, 'For the baby?'

'Yes.' She rushed into speech. 'I haven't knitted for years, but it's like riding a bicycle. I bought a really simple pattern, so it shouldn't be difficult to learn again. And yellow wool, in case—I mean, Benjy seems determined on a sister, but it might be a boy.

Do you think he'll mind?'

'No. Meredith, I'm sorry if I frightened you last night.'

Her eyes flew to his face. It was grim and his eyes looked worried.

She said, 'Not nearly as much as you frightened yourself.'

'Don't take any notice of my stupid ravings, will you? I was half asleep. I shouldn't have had so much to drink.'

'You hadn't been drinking the night before.'

He shrugged a little, shaking his head. 'Don't worry about it, anyway,' he said. 'Promise me.'

'All right.' She reached the end of the row, turned the needles, glancing down at the pattern, and said, 'Is it any use telling *you* not to worry?'

He smiled slightly. 'Husbands are entitled to. It's one of their natural functions.'

'It won't be like the last time,' she said in a low voice. 'There's no reason.'

'The odds against it must be astronomical,' he agreed. 'I know it won't happen again.

'But *do* you?' she asked, searching his face, the needles stilled. 'Really?'

'Really,' he said levelly. 'I'm not a neurotic idiot, darling. I don't actually believe in dreams and portents, and believe me, I'm no Cassandra. I don't think I've ever had a psychic experience in my life.'

She smiled a little absently. It wasn't quite what she was getting at, but she was still uncertain of her way. Her hands with the knitting in them dropped to her lap. She said jerkily, 'Simon, can we talk?'

He looked a little wary. 'Yes, of course.' He got up and switched off the television, creating an expectant silence, and stood with his back to it, apparently waiting, but his expression was shuttered.

She looked up at him, trying to find words, and he smiled wryly and said, 'I think I know what it's about, Meredith. I realise we can't go on living like—well, as we have been. And of course it's my fault. If it helps, I did see a doctor. He couldn't come up with a cause, but said it's probably very temporary and will come right of its own accord. And that worrying about it will only make matters worse.'

'It *isn't* your fault!' she said warmly.

He raised his brows. 'Well, it's hardly

yours.'

She shook her head. 'No, but I know you can't help it, Simon. I do understand.'

'Do you?' There was a hint of grim humour in his voice. 'Well, it's more than I do, then. I know we should have talked about it but I suppose I have the usual male hangups about potency and virility. All I really wanted to do was crawl into the nearest hole and hide my shame.'

'Oh, Simon!' she protested, putting aside the wool and the needles as she stood up and went over to him. Lifting her hand she touched his shoulder, stroking down his arm. 'That's silly. You don't have anything to be ashamed of.'

'That's what I tell myself. It doesn't help much, though. Feelings can't always be reasoned out of existence, no matter how silly they are.' He took her hand in his and looked down at it, then tugged her over to the sofa with him, retaining his hold while they sat side by side and half facing each other. 'Believe me, Meredith, I do want to make love to you. Sometimes quite desperately. Only—well——' He stopped with a wry little gesture. 'I suppose after what's been happening lately I'm afraid to try. It's humiliating for me, and it isn't fair to disappoint you.'

She kept her eyes fixed on him, her thoughts flying, darting. 'Simon,' she said tentatively, 'why were you so anxious for me not to start a baby?'

He seemed disconcerted. 'I told you the reasons,' he said, frowning. 'Several times.'

'Yes,' she said slowly, 'you had an awful lot of reasons.'

She tried to keep the bitterness out of her voice, but perhaps it showed in her eyes, because he avoided her gaze, making a slight, denying movement with his hand. 'I don't see that this has anything to do with what we're talking about.'

'But of course it does! It must have.'

'That's nonsense.' He stood up, going to stare out of the window, his hunched shoulder expressing rejection and extreme irritability.

Meredith suppressed a rising irritation of her own. He had said they would talk, but she knew that he was shutting her out, that deep inside himself was something that resented her probing. Yet it was important for her to know why he hadn't wanted the baby, why he wouldn't or couldn't accept it. And there *was* a connection. She knew it, and was stunned that he hadn't recognised it too. Her mind was ticking over rapidly, she felt like a person who was about to solve the last clue in a crossword puzzle, only needing the final letter or two to complete the vital word. She had to somehow breach the wall that seemed to have arisen between them. But Simon seemed determined to keep it intact. She looked at his rigid back and thought quite clearly that she wouldn't allow him retreat again behind the wall. 'When people give a lot of reasons for something,' she said, suddenly challenging, 'they're often hiding the real one.'

He twisted to look at her, his brows rising. 'Quite the little psychologist, aren't you? I told you before, it's not a field for amateurs.'

'Don't look down your nose at me like that,' she said tartly. 'It might have intimidated me when I was fourteen. Now it just makes me cross.'

'Well, the question's academic, isn't it?' he said, his hands thrust into his pockets. 'You're pregnant and there's nothing to be done about it now.'

He turned fully to look across the room at her. With his back to the window his face was shadowed. She couldn't read his expression, but his body had the tenseness that always showed when they discussed the coming baby.

Almost angrily she demanded, 'You've got to tell me the real reason you were so against it, Simon. Was it because of Jill?'

'What do you mean?' He went very still, his eyes narrowing, and she wished she hadn't said anything.

She hesitated, then decided it was too late to retract. 'Because she died having Benjy? *Were* you afraid of the same thing happening again?'

There was an instant's silence. He frowned, his mouth curling in derision and a kind of angry distaste. 'No, of course not!' he said shortly. 'That would be totally irrational.'

'Yes,' she agreed. 'It would. But what was that you said just now, about how feelings can't always be reasoned away?'

He moved impatiently and she said, '*Please*, Simon—think about it. I know you brushed me off when I suggested it before—refused to even consider the idea, but you *must*, now.

Do you remember how you reacted when I told you I was pregnant? I've never seen you so furious. Except——' she added, remembering, '—the day that Benjy went missing, and you threatened to tan his hide.'

'It wasn't the same thing at all. That was sheer fright,' he interjected.'

'Yes,' she said significantly. 'I know what it was.'

'You're being ridiculous!'

'I am not being ridiculous!' she said hotly, jumping to her feet, her eyes bright with the intensity of her emotion. 'For a man with a supposedly logical mind, you seem remarkably anxious to avoid thinking this thing through!'

'Which thing are we talking about now?' he enquired sarcastically. 'You seem to have changed the subject once or twice.'

'I don't think I have,' she told him, trying to be calm. 'I think it's all part of the same thing. And if you do love me, even a little, you'll at least try to do as I ask, and examine your own motives honestly.'

'Motives?'

'Don't you see?' she cried. 'The problem with sex has only arisen since I've been pregnant. You didn't want us to have a baby——'

'*Yet!*'

'All right!' she gestured impatiently. 'But you must see there's a connection. You know there is, if only you'll let yourself *think* about it.'

'What the hell else do you imagine I've been doing these last weeks?' he demanded.

'Well, maybe you've been on the wrong track!' she said, somewhat aggressively. 'You might at least listen to me! All I'm suggesting is that your reactions to Benjy's running away, and to my getting pregnant, were remarkably similar. Surely you must see that much?'

There was a long pause. His mouth was a hard line, a nerve jumping in his clenched jaw. She saw that he was controlling his temper, forcing his mind to take over. Then he said grudgingly, 'All right. You've got a point.' He prowled restlessly into the centre of the room. 'But it wasn't fear I felt when you told me you were pregnant.'

'What, then?' she prompted, and when he only moved his shoulder and jerked his head as though dismissing the question, her very silence demanded an answer. At length he said, with harsh reluctance, 'It was—a sort of violent, helpless rage.'

'Helpless?' she queried swiftly.

'For heaven's sake, don't pounce on my every word! I'd thought you were protected and it hadn't worked! I wasn't only furious with *you*! I felt guilty as hell too.'

'Why?'

'Because I shouldn't have left it all to you. I should have made sure you weren't taking stupid risks, that it was safe to——'

'Simon!' she protested. '*Listen* to yourself! Listen to the words you're using—protected; safe; *risks*! Don't you see? They're the words of *fear*.'

He drew in his breath savagely and she waited for a scorching denial. It didn't come. Instead, a hot flush of colour spread over his face and his lips clamped tightly for a few moments, his eyes fixed on hers while his brain absorbed what she had said, examined it unwillingly.

She watched him in silence, and he dragged his eyes from hers and stared moodily at the carpet. It was several minutes before he spoke again, and she listened with bated breath.

'The dream,' he muttered. '*That* was fear, what I felt in the dream.'

'Simon, can't you see——?' she almost whispered. 'The dream—wasn't it caused by your mind trying to push your subconscious feelings into the open and make you face them? In daylight, in your conscious mind, you know I'm not in any real danger. But at night, when your rational self is sleeping, those deepest feelings come to the surface.'

For a while he continued to stare at the floor. Then he looked at her and laughed a little, still with a kind of anger, but she thought she detected a hint of relief behind it. He said with light irony, 'I suppose you could be right. I bow to you, Madame Freud. I'd rather believe that, anyway, than that it was some kind of prophecy.'

'It wasn't a prophecy,' she said. It was only the fear that his conscious mind had denied, coming to the surface. And just as well, too, she thought. She went to him, hooking her arms about his neck. 'We can deal with it,' she said gently. For once he was less confident than she, caught off balance by the reluctant recognition of emotions he had buried so deeply that they only revealed themselves in dreams.

For seconds he was stiff and unyielding in her embrace. Then he pulled her close. 'All right, I'll buy your theory,' he said with some grimness. 'It probably does make a crazy kind of sense. It would explain the dreams, I suppose. Perhaps I do have some kind of subconscious, irrational dread that you—you might be as unlucky as Jill.' He paused. 'I don't see that it has anything to do with the more immediate problem, though. You're already pregnant, so . . . even my subconscious can't imagine I can save you now. It's too late.'

Her brain absorbed that, and reluctantly accepted his reasoning. Disappointment crushed her, and a hollow sickness started in her stomach. 'You're not repelled by pregnancy, are you?' she asked him, without much hope.

'Good lord, no!' He put her away from him a little and swept his eyes over the burgeoning curves of her body. 'If anything it makes you more beautiful.'

Hesitantly, she said, 'It's all right . . . if you can't feel the same about me as you did about Jill . . . if that's what's the matter.'

Simon looked stunned, his eyes narrowing with shock. 'What on earth are you talking about?'

'You didn't marry me because you'd fallen madly in love, and I know I've expected too much. I suppose I've been too—well, you know that I'm in love with you, but it doesn't matter if you don't—can't feel the same. Only I hope that some day, you—you might.'

He seemed thunderstruck. 'Meredith, I *love* you! I've told you often enough and I don't know any other way to say it!' He was grasping her shoulders, his eyes intensely blue.

'I know,' she sighed. 'But it's different, isn't it?'

'From what, for heaven's sake?'

'From the way you loved Jill.'

A frown appeared between his brows, and he shook his head as though to clear it. 'Of course it's *different*! I can't *compare* you and Jill—it's not possible! But I don't love you any *less*!'

'Oh, Simon!' Tears started in her eyes, and she heard her voice rise in a note of desperation. '*Please*, don't *lie* to me. It doesn't matter, so please don't tell me nice little lies.'

'*Meredith!*' He shook her suddenly,

speaking between his teeth. 'Will you *listen* to me, you little *idiot*!'

Her eyes widened, and he said unevenly, 'I'll try to explain. With Jill it was a bolt from the blue—I saw her and loved her, and I loved her until she died. With you—it crept up on me. Of course I'd loved you as a child, a friend, for years. I'd noticed how attractive you'd grown as a young woman, but it wasn't until the day I found you asleep—and I have a confession to make, I watched you for quite a long time before I woke you—that I realised that somewhere along the way I'd fallen in love, that I wanted you as my wife, to have and to hold for all the years to come, that I desired you as a woman, wanted to make love to you, to know your body over and over again. But—when I kissed you, you told me it was Michael you wanted.'

Michael's name brushed by her unnoticed. '*Then?*' she whispered, incredulous. 'You were in love with me *then*?'

He shook her again, but gently this time. 'No one else, idiot.'

'Stop calling me that,' she said automatically, but too filled with a growing hope to really care.

'It's what you are!' he said. 'How could you not *know*?'

'But you didn't tell me! You let me think it was all because of Michael!'

'I told you, all right, when I asked you to marry me, but you didn't seem very interested. I thought you knew the Sir Galahad act was motivated by enlightened self-interest. Altruistic I may be, but marrying a girl I didn't want just to save her from a sticky social situation is carrying it a bit far! I was prepared to wait for you to get over Michael, but I still had some pride left. I wasn't going to continually throw my heart at the feet of a woman who at the time couldn't have cared less for it.'

'But I thought——'

'What?'

'Well, that you'd just decided that I'd do. I mean, you wanted a proper home for Benjy, and a wife, and just about anyone would have done as long as she realised that—that your heart wasn't hers.'

'My heart is yours, Meredith,' he said. 'And anything else you want that it's in my power to give you.'

'But,' she said doubtfully, moistening her

lips, 'you didn't want to give me a baby.'

'I didn't want to lose you,' he said huskily. 'I think I must admit that you were right about that. I couldn't bear the slightest risk for you. Doesn't that prove that I do love you, in all the ways there are?'

'Then . . . why?'

He pulled her fully into his arms, his hand on her hair, his cheek against her temple. 'I don't know why!' he said, with a hint of despair. 'I love you, I want you . . . terribly. I just don't understand why my body won't let me make love to you.'

'I thought it was guilt . . . that you felt you were being unfaithful to Jill,' she said, her voice muffled.

'No,' he said positively, his arms tightening about her. 'Nothing like that. The only thing I had to be guilty about was putting you in danger . . .'

His voice trailed off, as though his words had surprised himself, and Meredith lifted her head from his chest and looked at him, her eyes wide, seeing the dawning comprehension in his face that matched her own.

'If you felt like that,' she said softly, putting both their thoughts into words, 'and you were afraid of what could happen to me, mightn't that interfere with your reflexes?'

He suddenly shook with laughter, and she said, 'What's funny? I'm putting forward a perfectly serious psychological theory.'

'You,' he said. ' "Interfere with my reflexes"! Where did you pick up stuff like that? At the hospital?'

'I suppose so.' She smiled sheepishly. 'Does it sound like terrible jargon?'

'Terrible. But, oh God, I love you!' He crushed her in his arms, his cheek against hers, and held her there for long moments, until she stirred and turned her head and met his mouth as it sought hers.

'Well,' he said after a long while, 'now that you've sorted out all my psychological hangups, what's the next step?'

'I think,' she said, judiciously, her eyes beginning to dance, 'a controlled experiment might be in order. How would you feel about having your reflexes tested?'

A flicker of something she couldn't read entered his eyes and she held her breath. His grip tightened. 'Are you sure?' he asked her.

'I'm sure,' she said. She pulled his mouth down to hers again and deliberately moved her body against him. His breath caught, and his hands went to her hips and brought her even closer. 'It might not work,' he said, doubt in his voice.

'It doesn't matter. It's going to be all right, I'm certain of it. If not tonight, then sometime soon. We've got all our lives, Simon. And I promise you, that's a long, long time.'

He tipped her head back with his hands and kissed her deeply and thoroughly until she was breathless and flushed, clinging to his shoulders to keep her balance. 'It will never be long enough,' he said, 'to show you how much I love you.'

'When are we going to cut baby's cake?' Benjy asked, leaning on the bed as Meredith did up the front of her dress and lifted her baby daughter to her shoulder.

'Soon,' she promised. 'And baby has a name now.'

'I know. Elisa Kathryn. Can I hold her?'

'Sit on the bed, then. Put your arm under her head.'

Simon tapped on the door and came in. 'Nearly ready?' he asked. 'I've had to stop several of our guests from barging in here to get another look at our daughter, and my mother's hovering round the table, ready to cut the christening cake.'

'Can Elisa have some?' Benjy asked.

'She's too little,' Meredith told him. 'But she won't mind if you eat her slice.'

She got off the bed and bent to take the baby.

'Go and tell Oma we'll be there in a minute, would you?' Simon said to Ben, and stopped Meredith with a hand on her arm as she made to go after the boy.

He looked down at the sleeping baby, then bent to kiss Meredith. 'You both look beautiful,' he said. 'I'm the luckiest man alive.'

'You look good, too,' she told him. She sometimes thought her pregnancy had been a greater strain on him than on her. She knew he had tried to rationalise his fear out of existence, but every so often she had caught a shadow of strain in his expression. Not until after she had left the hospital, had it completely disappeared. 'And I'm the luckiest woman,' she added softly.

Simon smiled. 'Flattery will get you everywhere. Especially into bed.'

'I'll look forward to it,' she promised demurely. 'But right now we have more important things to do, like cutting this cake.'

He slapped her softly as she passed him, and they went out into the lounge to be met by claps and cheers.

They cut the cake with Ben's help on Elisa's behalf, while Anneke held her godchild, and then Simon thanked everyone for taking part in the christening.

'And here's to many more!' one of the Dutch uncles called, to gales of laughter.

Meredith looked up at Simon and met his questioning eyes. 'Yes,' she said.

He smiled. 'If that's what you want.'

There was no shadow behind his smile, and she knew that at last he was free of the dark, haunting shadow of the past. He handed her a glass of champagne as someone proposed a toast to their daughter, and they drank to their future together.

THESE ARE THE OTHER TITLES
TO LOOK OUT FOR
THIS MONTH

TIME FUSE
by Penny Jordan

On the day Selina accepted a job working for the father she had never seen before, she lit a fuse she had no way of controlling. But it wasn't her father who was the cause of the explosion — but his nephew Piers, who made no secret of his desire, and contempt for her!

A MOMENT IN TIME
by Yvonne Whittal

Christie's excitement at her new job was dashed when Lyle Venniker turned up as her boss. But why did he hate her so much? Hadn't she given him what he wanted — his freedom?

EACH MONTH MILLS & BOON PUBLISH
THREE LARGE PRINT ROMANCES
FOR YOU TO LOOK OUT FOR,
AND ENJOY. THESE ARE THE TITLES
FOR NEXT MONTH

———————— * ————————

MIDWIFE MELANIE
by Kate Ashton

SEPARATE LIVES
by Caroline Jantz

THE WILDER SHORES OF LOVE
by Madeleine Ker